W9-ACR-883

Deadly Resurrection

Deadly Resurrection

James T. Doyle

ASBURY PARK PUBLIC LIBRARY
ASBURY PARK, NEW JERSEY

Walker and Company
New York

Copyright © 1987 by James T. Doyle

All rights reserved. No part of this book may be reproduced
or transmitted in any form or by any means, electronic or
mechanical, including photocopying, recording, or by any
information storage and retrieval system, without permission
in writing from the Publisher.

All the characters and events portrayed in this story are
fictitious.

First published in the United States of America in 1987 by the
Walker Publishing Company, Inc.

Published simultaneously in Canada by John Wiley & Sons
Canada, Limited, Rexdale, Ontario.

Library of Congress Cataloging-in-Publication Data

Doyle, James T., 1928–
    Deadly resurrection.

    I. Title.
PS3554.09744D4   1987   813'.54   86-24714
ISBN 0-8027-5669-7

Printed in the United States of America

10 9 8 7 6 5 4 3 2 1

For Betty,
  Who knows all the reasons why.

Deadly Resurrection

1

MURRAY ATWOOD STARED up at me with dead eyes.

He wasn't a pretty sight sitting there on the couch with his throat and chest a bloody mess. His head rested crookedly on the back of the couch. His right hand lay limply in his lap. The other one, palm down, stretched out beside him on the seat cushion.

I could only assume that it was Atwood, since I had never met him. The name on the door of the apartment, however, said Atwood, and the corpse in front of me wore slippers on its feet. I figured that justified my assumption.

I looked for his telephone and found it in the bedroom. I used my handkerchief to hold the receiver and my pen to dial the number of my office. Only my client would be there to answer it. I supposed that she would.

She picked up the phone on the sixth ring, her voice sounding a little tentative. I told her to sit tight until I got back.

"Is something wrong?"

I saw no point in ducking the issue. "Someone shot your boyfriend dead," I replied.

She gasped. After the gasp I heard only the sound of her breathing. She must have been thinking over this new complication in her life.

"Did you get the letters?" she asked.

"Forget the letters."

"But . . ."

"Dammit, I haven't time to argue. The cops have to know about this, and I need to know how to play it."

"Please, not the police. I . . ."

"Shut up," I told her. "Right now my problem is bigger than yours. Three people got a good look at me on my way into the building. If I don't call the police and if I don't wait for them, I'll be suspect number one."

"They don't know who you are," she pleaded. She sounded miserably afraid. I wished I could have helped, but it wouldn't have helped either of us for me to go to jail.

"This is a small building. The people who saw me know that I'm a stranger. I could have dropped a fingerprint or two. I don't know. You didn't tell me to expect a corpse, so maybe I was careless."

"You don't think that I killed him?" Something that sounded like the beginnings of hysteria crept into her voice.

"Did you?"

She uttered little moaning sounds over the phone. I demanded an answer. I heard her take in a deep breath. When she spoke, she had her voice under control.

"No. I did not kill him. What good would that have done me?"

If she had killed Atwood, I would have expected her to lie. I wasn't listening to her words, only to the steady assurance in her voice. It wasn't much to go on, but it was all I had at the moment.

I repeated my order to stay in the office until my return and hung up the phone. She'd wait until I had completed my civic duty. She had no choice. I still had her ten thousand dollars. Atwood wouldn't be needing it now.

2

2

You don't have to be a genius to be a private detective, at least not in my town, Washington, D.C., but you're supposed to know enough not to flee the scene of a murder, unless you did the killing. That was a conclusion I did not want the metropolitan police to jump to, so my next call was to Third District headquarters.

After that I went back to the living room. I told my stomach to behave and considered the corpse once more. Atwood must have been dead a while. The drying of his blood seemed well advanced. I went very carefully around the coffee table and ventured the back of my hand against his cheek. It felt cool, almost cold. If distance could not supply me with an alibi, time would have to do. I had arrived at Atwood's apartment barely five minutes earlier. Death had visited there at least an hour before that.

I looked around the room. A revolver lay on the carpet a little apart from the coffee table. It looked like a thirty-two. It's difficult to say from eight feet away, which was as close as I wanted to get to that gun.

The light oak-colored wood of the coffee table matched the exposed arms of the couch and of the two easy chairs. Two small matching tables stood beside each chair. Lamps with jar-shaped blue ceramic bases lit the room. The draperies across the window had been pulled shut. Under the window, a hot-water radiator worked to fend off the December afternoon's chill.

On the coffee table, four magazines were neatly arranged in a single pile. A cigar had died in the ashtray, its ash undisturbed. Atwood's wristwatch lay next to the ashtray. The time on it agreed with my watch. Two glasses stood on opposite sides of the table. The one closest to Atwood was nearly empty; the other, nearly full. Atwood, it was obvious, had not expected violent death.

I went to the kitchen and from there to the bedroom and then to the bathroom. I gave each a quick visual survey before going back to the living room. The whole apartment was neat and orderly. I saw no sign either of the packet of letters or of anyone's having searched the apartment before my arrival.

A heavy rapping at Atwood's door announced the arrival of the nearest patrol officers dispatched to the scene. They were polite. They asked me to stand aside after they took my name and address and saw my identification. Two homicide branch detectives, with technicians in tow, arrived shortly. The technicians set up shop while one of the detectives, Detective Paddock, he said he was, took command.

He was a short, solid-looking man. His hair was cut close around his neck and ears, longer on top. It gave his head an impression of squareness, an impression heightened by his flat cheeks and angular jaw. He stood behind one of the armchairs, looking down at the corpse, hands thrust deeply into the pockets of his blue raincoat. He turned and appraised me with hard, black eyes.

"Who's he?" he asked the patrolman.

"Private eye, by name of Dan Cronyn," answered the cop, a big, pudgy-cheeked rookie, or close to it. "He called it in. He was here when we got here."

"Been over him yet?" asked Paddock.

The young cop confessed he had not.

"Then do it," snapped Paddock and turned back to his study of the corpse.

I've been frisked before, and it's no big deal. The

rookie took it slow and careful. When he finished, he told the other detective, one called Karle, that I was clean. Karle who was thin and looked out at the world with a pinched expression on his face, seemed barely interested. I was mainly in the way at that point.

"Take him out in the hall," he told the rookie before turning to me and saying, "Like to have you stick around a while, Cronyn."

He wasn't asking me; he was telling me. "Don't forget me," I said and followed the patrol officer out to the hall.

Three other uniformed cops loafed there. My pudgy-cheeked guardian ignored me to join his colleagues at the head of the stairs at the rear of the building. Atwood had lived in 3-D, which meant his apartment was in the front. I could look out the hall window to the street and see the flashing red lights of the metropolitan police cruisers on the street below.

A small crowd had gathered on the sidewalk. A woman saw me at the window and pointed up. I turned away and ignored the gapers. Directly across the hall from me was 3-A. At the rear of the building were the other two apartments on that floor, 3-B and 3-C. When I had consulted the mailboxes on the first floor, the name slot for 3-C was empty. I suspected that the apartment was also empty.

Eventually they came for me, Paddock this time. He took me into Atwood's apartment past the corpse and into the bedroom. There was a bed covered by a plain gold spread in the room, also a five-drawer chest and mirrored dresser made of the same light oak as the living-room furniture. The whole apartment looked as though it had been furnished by a rental outlet.

Paddock shut the door and told me to sit on the bed. A plain wood chair with a plastic seat stood in the corner of the room. He pulled it out, turned its back to face me, and sat down, draping his arms over its back.

"How'd ja get in?" he asked.

"The door was ajar," I told him.

"You make a habit of walking into any apartment with an open door?" Paddock asked. "I'm surprised that we haven't met before."

I ignored the sarcasm. "Atwood was expecting me."

"He's a good friend?"

"Never saw him before tonight. It was business."

"Tell me about it."

"I'd like to keep my client out of this."

He laughed without humor, showing me his teeth. "Don't give me that shit, cowboy. You either spill your guts, or you go into the tank."

"You have to have a charge for that."

"I'll think of something."

I didn't doubt it, but I tried to talk him out of it. "You couldn't hold me on a hummer, Detective Paddock," I said, trying to be polite by remembering his name. "It would have to be something more substantial than that."

"Want to try me?" he asked, stretching his lips in a fake smile.

"No," I admitted. He could take me in on a trumped-up charge, and it could cause me a lot of trouble. I didn't need another arrest on my record, if it could be avoided. I thought it could.

"My client's a woman," I said, not wanting to spend the night, or longer, in the city jail. "Atwood had some of her letters. She wanted them back. She hired me to make the deal."

"Why you? What's so special about you, cowboy?"

"I'm in the Yellow Pages. She let her fingers do the walking and they stopped at me. Just lucky, I guess." I had not meant my response to sound flippant but I guess it did. Paddock didn't like it.

"Nobody likes a smart-ass," he said. "Especially one who advertises." He took out his notebook and a ballpoint pen. "So who's the woman?"

I hesitated. There's nothing in the How-to-be-a-Private-Detective book that says you have to shield a client, but you assume that the client came to you in the first place in order to avoid the police.

"Thick-headed, that's what you are," Paddock went on, noticing my hesitation. "How about suspicion of murder? Is your client paying enough to cover the cost of your lawyer and the bondsman's tab?"

Thus encouraged, I suggested that he might want to talk to Pamela Davidson. I gave him the Crystal City address and the telephone number. I added a cautionary note as he wrote the information on a small pad of paper.

"It might be a phony," I said. "I checked the Virginia telephone directory on my way over here and didn't find a listing for a Pamela Davidson or for any Davidson at that address. Of course, the phone could be unlisted."

"You sure are gullible, cowboy," he said. "You believe everything you're told?"

"I believed the ten thousand she showed me. She was ready to make a deal. Her name could have been Santa Claus for all I cared."

His black eyes rounded and glittered darkly. "Those letters must be pretty important," he said.

"They were to her. She told me that Atwood was ready to deal. She wanted me to negotiate the price."

"You have the money with you?"

I decided to start lying at that point. Ten one-thousand-dollar bills lay quietly in my wallet. The cop who frisked me hadn't seen them because he was looking for a weapon, not money.

"No," I replied to his question. "She wanted me to negotiate the price. She said that she would call me tomorrow and give me the money to make the exchange."

In fact, she had said exactly that. What I did not tell Paddock was that I had talked her out of doing it that way.

Paddock looked at me with deep suspicion in his eyes.

"And give Atwood a chance to think about it over-night?" he said. "Dangle the cash in front of a black-mailer and they'll grab for it. Give them a chance to think it over and they'll double their price."

He stated the argument I had used to persuade the reluctant Pamela Davidson to part with her ten thou. To her I had added the refusal to do it any other way. If Atwood agreed to deal, I wanted to finish it. In the end she handed over her money.

I shrugged at Paddock. "Sure," I said. "I told her that, but she insisted on doing it her way."

"Uh-huh," said Paddock, still suspicious. He stood up and went out of the bedroom for a minute or two and came back and sat down again in the chair. He stared at me for a long time. It was supposed to make me uncom-fortable. It did. That's the trouble with lies. Unless you're accomplished at it, suspicion can make you feel uncomfortable. Paddock's suspicion showed.

"What did you do with the letters?" he asked me.

"I haven't seen them."

"You looked the place over after you killed Atwood, didn't you?"

"I didn't kill Atwood. You know that."

"I do?" He put his notebook and pen back in his raincoat pocket. "What did you do with the letters?"

"Nothing. I don't have the letters."

"We had better find them here, in that case," he warned me. "But then you've already looked, haven't you?"

"I called in as soon as I found the body," I replied. "I figured that you guys would turn up the letters if I told you about them."

"Yeah. Sure." His voice carried disbelief in it. Then he started at the beginning, and we went through the same dance again. When we finished that, he started at the end, and we went through it backwards.

"You figured that we'd turn up the letters, all right," he said, "when you couldn't. If you'd have found them, they'd be ashes down the toilet, right?"

"You can make your own guesses."

He smiled a little when he heard the annoyance in my voice. The smile had no warmth in it. Neither did his eyes. He uncoiled himself from his chair and walked over to the bed and looked down at me. His face still held tightly to that cold smile.

"Get up," he ordered.

I thought I knew what was coming. I hesitated in standing. He knew what I was thinking, and his smile broadened by a hair. He repeated the order to stand. It would have to be standing, of course. He'd want his fist to go into my belly, where it wouldn't hurt him, not on my head or jaw, where he could break a hand.

"Can't take it, eh, smart-ass? All mouth and no guts," he said. "That's good to know."

I stood up and looked down at him. I tried to tighten my stomach muscles for the impact. My eyes never left those rock-hard orbs glinting out at me. I didn't say anything. I just stood up and waited.

"Well, how about that?" he said. "Maybe your balls aren't made of jelly, after all."

"You're bluffing, Paddock, and you know it. That sort of thing went out with the rubber hose."

"That's right, smart-ass. Hell, everybody knows that, don't they? Except that everybody isn't in this room, just you and me."

The door opened. The other detective came in. He popped something into his mouth between thin lips and chewed on it. If he partnered all the time with Paddock, I'd bet it was a Rolaid. He stood looking at the two of us, surveying the scene, hitching narrow shoulders in an attitude of casual nonconcern. His glance wound up on Paddock.

9

"Rowlson's here," he said.

"Ain't we lucky," Paddock said. He went back to his chair and sat down. "Put your ass back on the bed, cowboy."

I sat down. The door opened again and a tall, slender man in a gray suit came into the room. His face showed high cheek bones and regular features. His skin had the soft sheen and color of chestnut.

"Hello, Al," he said, addressing himself to Paddock in a voice which showed no trace of the street in it. He looked me over. "He found the victim?"

"That's right, Lieutenant," said Paddock. "He called in." Paddock asked the other detective if he'd found anyone to confirm my story.

"A woman on the first floor saw him come in. She was standing at the mailboxes right by the front door. A man and a woman on the second floor saw him come up the stairs and head on up to this third floor. They all agreed that he arrived about ten, maybe fifteen, minutes before the first officers on the scene."

I offered silent thanks to the observant and public-spirited tenants of Northwest Gardens.

Rowlson didn't seem too interested in me or in Murray Atwood. His questions to his two detectives, mainly to Paddock, had to do with such things as response times and cooperation from the patrol officers and the adequacy of technical support services. Rowlson hadn't come to solve the murder of Murray Atwood, only to see if the men in his organization were doing the things they were trained to do, the things that experience proved offered the best chance of finding and convicting the killer.

Rowlson's only question to me was to ask if I'd been told my rights.

"I think that Detective Paddock was just getting around to that when you arrived, Lieutenant," I told him.

10

Rowlson stayed for that and then left, accompanied out of the bedroom by Paddock's partner.

"It's your lucky night, cowboy," observed Paddock. "Now forget that Miranda crap and talk to me. You could have been here earlier and taken care of Atwood."

"Why would I come back?"

"I don't know. Why did you?"

"I didn't."

"Maybe you panicked earlier. Then you remembered leaving the gun and came back for it."

"I told you what I came for."

"Yeah. We got a little problem with that, cowboy. So far we haven't come across any letters."

"Maybe Atwood kept them somewhere else. They were worth money to him. He could keep them in a safe-deposit box."

"Only you said that he was ready to make a deal. If he was ready to make a deal, why didn't he have the merchandise here? Doesn't that strike you funny, cowboy?"

I didn't see anything funny about it. It worried me. I expected the cops would have found the letters routinely and certainly after I told Paddock about them.

"Do you have a permit to carry iron?"

"I do," I replied, "but I seldom carry. I prefer to avoid taking on a case where I might need a gun."

"So you wouldn't know anything about the piece laying on the floor in the other room?"

"That's right," I replied.

Paddock stood up and went to the door and called a question into the living room. "It's a thirty-two," someone answered.

Paddock came back to his chair, sat down, and looked at me. "Own a thirty-two?" he asked.

"No," I replied. "Are we about finished?"

"When I say so."

"You have it all."

Paddock considered me carefully for a third of a minute. "Got a record?" he asked me.

I hesitated, and he prompted me. "Well? I can find out, you know. What will I find when I look?"

"Not much," I told him. "I ran into a nightstick in Chicago in 1968, during the Democratic Convention. I bled a lot in front of some TV cameras. You know what a split eyebrow is like. I made the evening news and wound up with a splitting headache and three days in jail."

Paddock eyed me with distaste. "A goddamned radical."

"Yeah," I assured him. "You'll find an arrest for possession of marijuana. I got busted during a nice peaceful sit-in. That was in 1969. I had two joints in my pocket, and I was dragging on the one in my hand. Had me cold, but the judge was trying to prove his liberal credentials so that his wife could get invited to some radical-chic affairs. He threw out the case and called it police harassment. Finally, the FBI picked me up for conspiracy. That really was harassment, and it never went to trial."

"How in the hell did you get a private eye's license?" exploded Paddock.

"No convictions," I told him, truthfully. "Zip. Besides, all that's been a long time ago, Paddock. A lifetime ago."

He didn't let me go right away. He kept me around for his partner to go over the same ground that he had already covered three times. I considered it harassment, but maybe it's just the way they do things. My time wasn't entirely wasted, however; I learned a few things.

The two glasses I saw on Atwood's coffee table each contained an alcoholic beverage, probably Scotch whiskey, according to Paddock's partner, which had been diluted wtih either water or ice or both. Both glasses had fingerprints on them, the one almost certainly Atwood's. It would take a day or two before they knew whether they could match the prints on the other glass with the prints on file. It was, at the moment, their best lead, but homicide detectives are a phlegmatic lot not given to exaggerated expectations.

None of the neighbors had heard the shots, or if they had heard them they did not identify them as shots and so had not remembered them. The neighbor across the hall from Atwood thought she heard a car backfire sometime during the afternoon, but she had no idea when that might have occurred. As I had earlier surmised, 3-C, the apartment next to Atwood's, was vacant. The woman in 2-D, directly under Atwood's place, had been at work.

The killer had emptied all six shots from the thirty-two into Atwood, probably in rapid succession. Time was when somebody would surely have heard six bullets fired from a revolver. Since then, however, television, quadra-phonic sound, and Walkman have been invented, and nobody hears anything anymore except their own self-inflicted noise pollution.

Paddock came back and grudgingly admitted that he had found no sign I had searched the apartment. Apparently no one had, but the cops could turn up no letters either. Atwood's dresser contained a few receipts and five hundred dollars in cash, but no checkbook. Detective Karle hypothesized that maybe Atwood had been doing some shoplifting and based his idea on the half-dozen shopping bags found in Atwood's closet, all from Woodward and Lothrop, the big local department-store chain.

Paddock was skeptical. "So how come," he asked Karle, "they're all from Woodies? He had something against stealing from Hecht's or Garfinkel's?"

Karle conceded the point but clung to the notion and said he'd have it checked and went out of the room.

Paddock shook his head and turned to me and told me, finally, that I could go. He added, "I'll be seeing you again, cowboy." The tightness in his voice betrayed an inner strain, a spring wound to its snapping point. I told myself to remember that.

"And, Cronyn," he continued, black eyes glittering, "you better hope that we find those letters."

With that hope as an incentive, I legged it back to the spot where I had left my station wagon and headed it toward my F Street office and my client.

3

I WALKED IN on her while she was in the act of using my telephone. She had settled herself in my chair. When she saw me she stood up and turned away toward the window. She murmured into the phone with her hand cupped around the mouthpiece. She obviously had no intention of sharing the conversation with me.

While she finished murmuring into the phone, I went to the water cooler and filled a five-ounce paper cup with water. I carried it to the desk along with an empty one.

The desk and chairs were wood, built in the earlier part of the century and come from a government-surplus sale. So had the battered steel file cabinets, still with the bar locks. It would take a good man about two minutes to get into those cabinets and leave them looking like they'd never been touched. If he didn't care about appearances, it would probably take him thirty seconds.

In any event, he wouldn't find much. The juicy stuff, the stuff that a Washington, D.C., investigator is bound to turn up by the time he's been in business for ten years, slept peacefully in a box in the underground vault of the National Bank of Washington, a few blocks away.

There wasn't much else in the single room I operated out of. On the walls were four chalk drawings, presents from the artist, a girl who had lived with me for six months a few years back. She had subsequently gone on to acquire some modest fame in the art world. As a consequence of that fame, I supposed that the drawings were worth something, but I prized them more for their sentimental value. They reminded me of her and of cold, white wine and of warm, dark nights and of a feeling that was probably love. Neither of us recognized it then, and so we lost it to what we thought we wanted, instead of holding on to what we had.

The rest of the room didn't amount to much. A thousand might cover everything else in it: typewriter, calculator, telephone-answering apparatus, and all the odds and ends, including the rented water cooler in the corner. I didn't have a whole lot of money tied up in my business. Just part of my life.

Pamela Davidson closed off her conversation, put the handset down gently, and turned to face me. She was an attractive-looking woman and old enough to be interesting, which to me means that she was past thirty. I couldn't be sure how far past. It didn't look like much, but if I had to bet on it I would have gone against the external evidence and said that she was halfway to forty. It must have been something in her eyes, something that said she knew more than most of us do at any age. It was just a feeling I had. On the surface, she was just another reasonably attractive married woman looking ahead to forty and beginning to wonder what she was missing out of life. So she tasted the forbidden fruit and now needed me to get her out of the jam.

She moved around my old wooden desk and stood before me. She filled out her black ribnecked sweater in the places where it looked the best. Below she wore gray slacks of soft wool.

"I thought . . ." she began, changed her mind, and tried again. "I didn't know what to think."

"Sorry. I couldn't call." I went around my desk and sat down.

"The police?"

"That's right," I said. "The police. Let's talk."

"I must get back," she said, "before my husband comes home from his office."

I motioned to the phone. "That was him?"

"Yes."

"He's been in his office all day?"

She blinked. "I don't know." She straightened up. "Why?"

"Didn't it ever occur to you that your husband may have found out about your love affair and taken care of your lover himself?"

She paused for a long moment. "I suppose that it's possible. Anything is possible."

She hesitated. Then, "May I have my money back now?"

Ten thousand bucks concentrates the mind wonderfully. Lover boy might be no more than a bloody mess gone cold, but the ten thou was alive and well and only three arms' lengths away from her.

"In a minute," I said. I wanted some answers, and those answers were the price she'd have to pay for getting her money back. It seemed like a bargain, after what I'd been through.

"What is your real name, Mrs. Davidson? We'll start with that."

She obviously didn't want to start with anything at all, but she was in no position to argue. "My name is Paula Devlin," she said.

"You're sure?"

She took no offense at my skepticism. She opened her purse and removed a card case and pushed it across the top of the desk toward me.

It was a nice case, red leather on the outside. The inside had individual compartments for a half-dozen or so cards, not the kind of plastic insert that falls out like toilet paper unrolling when you open it. All the cards and the driver's license said Paula Devlin. The picture on the driver's license wasn't too flattering but it definitely was the woman in front of me.

I handed the card case back to her. "Whiskey?" I

17

offered. I rose and went to the file cabinet where I kept the office bottle, mainly for clients who needed it. This time I needed it more than the client. She declined, but I helped myself, filling a paper cup with the stuff. I went back to the desk, sat down, and pulled her ten thousand from my wallet. I placed the bills on my desk blotter.

She watched me without comment.

"When did you last see Murray Atwood?"

"The day before yesterday," she replied. "Saturday."

"At his place?" I asked. She nodded. I went on. "Did anyone see you?"

"I don't know. I suppose so."

"You'd been there before, for trysts?"

She avoided my eyes. "Yes. Several times."

"Often enough that the neighbors might have seen you and remembered you?"

"I suppose so," she said, some defiance in her voice. "What difference does it make?"

"The cops will be interested in everybody who knows Murray Atwood, including his girlfriend." I paused. "Especially an ex-girlfriend, betrayed and blackmailed."

"I didn't kill Murray Atwood."

"Yeah," I replied. You'd expect her to deny it, sure. It made no difference whether I believed her or not. "The last time you saw him, did he have the letters in his apartment?"

"Yes. He called me Friday night. He said that he wanted the money right away, that he had to leave town. I went there Saturday to try to plead with him. I tried to remind him of what we had once meant to each other." She stopped, as though to recall a memory, looking away once more. She swung her glance back to me. Her face hardened. "It all came down to a question of money, Mr. Cronyn. According to him, he needed it, and I had it. What could be simpler?"

"Did you see the letters?"

"Yes."

"Were they in their envelopes?"

"No. Just bundled together with a rubber band."

"Had you signed them with your full name?"

"No. Just with a P. He said that it made no difference. The handwriting was mine. That was enough to prove me a liar if I tried to deny them. I knew that I had to get them. That's why I came to you. It's not important now, is it?"

"The letters haven't been found in his apartment, so you have to ask yourself, if he didn't have them there two days ago, who took them away?"

She gave me a blank look. "Who would want them?"

"Someone who thought that they might be worth ten thou," I told her. "Did Atwood ever mention suspecting that someone who knew you might have known about your affair?"

She thought it over carefully before giving her answer. "We never talked about the people I knew."

"That doesn't mean he might not know your friends. A blackmailer would want first to know how vulnerable you are before investing his time in you," I pointed out. "What did he do for a living?"

She lifted her shoulders helplessly. "I don't know. We never talked about it."

"What the hell did you talk about? You couldn't have spent all your time . . ." I stopped abruptly. Walking in on a corpse, getting grilled by the cops, and not knowing what to do next was making me irritable. I had to remind myself that it wasn't her fault. She hadn't gotten me into it. It was part of the risks of the job. If a baker doesn't like how much heat his ovens create, he ought to find a new line of work, not blame the customer who likes fresh rolls.

"Forget it," I said. "Right now the spotlight is on you and me. I'd like to give the police someone else to chew on. If no one else knew about those letters, that leaves only you. You had a good reason to pop Atwood, the best. Woman scorned and betrayed."

"I didn't kill him."

"So you told me."

"Why would I come here, if I had done it?"

"Maybe you figured that you could pull something fancy with the time of death, like breaking his watch or clock after setting it at a phony time. Or setting the thermostat high so the body wouldn't cool so fast or putting the air conditioner on so it would cool faster."

She just stared at me, as though she didn't know what the hell I was talking about. She hadn't done any of those things, of course. There had been no smashed clocks. Atwood's wristwatch lay undisturbed on the coffee table. The temperature in the apartment was what you'd have expected. I was trying to squeeze her piece of the puzzle into an opening where it wouldn't fit. But if Atwood had those letters with him, ready to make a deal, someone had to have taken them.

It still didn't fit her, no matter how I turned it around. If he had the letters there, hidden, she'd have had to search for them. Neither I nor the cops had seen any sign of a search, certainly not by an amateur in a hurry because a murder had just been committed.

I turned the puzzle in another direction, trying out the possibility that he had the letters right there in the room in plain view, on the coffee table perhaps. That wouldn't fit either. If she had a gun in her hand, she didn't have to kill to get the letters.

A struggle then. She makes a grab for the letters and he makes a grab for her. A gun is within her reach. Bang-bang.

Nuts-nuts.

Whoever shot Atwood stood directly across the coffee table from him. It would have called for an exceedingly dainty struggle to the death not to have disturbed the contents of that table. A fiendishly cool and clever murderer might try to straighten up later, but not even the steadiest of hands could have put the ash back on the end of Atwood's cigar.

I stood up and went back to the water cooler. My mouth remained curiously dry. Maybe corpses have that effect on me. Every death reminds one of how quickly the brief light of life can pass into the one everlasting night that waits for all of us.

I drew a cupful of water and turned back to face her, speaking at her from across the room.

"Okay," I told her. "You didn't kill him." She looked relieved. That was premature. "The letters," I reminded her. "Someone has to have them. They didn't get up and walk away."

She shook her head. "I don't care."

"You'd better care, lady. For both our sakes. Just because I think you're innocent doesn't mean the cops will. Suppose they get the idea that you and I are working together? That you killed him, and I went back and got the letters and managed to get rid of them?"

She bit her lip. That last possibility hit her where it hurt. She took a moment to think it over. She wanted to deny the possibility, even in her own mind.

"They couldn't think that," she said, half a hope forming her words. "They have no reason."

"They can manufacture reasons," I said. "You can't afford to appear unconcerned about where those letters are, and I can't either. Otherwise the police will start thinking that we don't care because we know where they are or where they went or both. That leads to questions about how we got them away from Atwood."

I poured a little of the Scotch into a fresh cup, added an equal amount of water, and shoved it across the desk toward her. She looked as though she could use it.

I spoke again. "You haven't seen Atwood since the day before yesterday?"

"No. He gave me today as a deadline. Either I had the money for him by this afternoon, or he would send one of the letters to my husband. I had no choice but to pay."

"Why bring me into it?"

"I didn't trust him. He might have taken the money from me and refused to give me the letters. What could I have done? That's why I called you this morning. I had made up my mind that, if I had to pay, I was going to have those letters back."

"But they're still missing."

"Yes," she replied in a small voice, looking down.

"I'm going to find them," I told her.

Her eyes came up quickly. "No," she said. "Please just leave it alone."

I shook my head. "I understand how you feel, Mrs. Devlin, but you aren't out of the woods yet. The person who took those letters may be the same person who put Atwood away."

"You'd turn the letters over to the police, wouldn't you?" I didn't answer. She went on. "My husband would throw me out," she said, "without anything." She looked at the cash spread out on my desk blotter. "May I have my money now?"

I pushed the ten thousand in cash across the desk to her. She put it in her purse and stood up.

"Sit down," I said. "We're not quite finished."

"I've got to get home."

"Not before you tell me something about Murray Atwood. And about you."

She sat back down, making no attempt to hide her impatience. "I don't know anything about Murray. I've already told you that."

"About you, in that case."

I had to prime her with some questions to get her

started, but after the beginning it came fast. She was in a hurry.

She'd been married to Walter Devlin for eight years, she said. It was, I gathered, a comfortable relationship and one she wanted to hold on to. She freely admitted that she had not been in love with Devlin when she married him. There was another reason for her commitment to the marriage, one that some women find equally as compelling as love.

"Walter makes a great deal of money," she said.

She had no family, no brothers to avenge the honor lost to Murray Atwood, nor anyone else apparently. She seemed always to have been pretty much a loner before coming to Washington and meeting her Prince Charming. She'd lived in a number of places, it seemed, before settling down. Well, I'd already decided that she wasn't a bad-looking woman, and she was intelligent and had a certain undefinable quality about her that some very interesting women have. It was only a matter of time until she met a man whose marriage proposal made economic sense to her.

"Do you think that your husband might have known about Atwood?"

She had to think about that. "I don't know," she answered. "I can't recall any indication of it, but Walter is very clever."

"The ones who make a lot of money often are. Clever enough to have known about your affair without giving you any indication that he knew?" She nodded.

"He'd have ways of dealing with the situation?"

"Yes."

I didn't ask what those ways might be, but maybe they included murder. So all right, I now had one possibility, someone who had a believable motive for dispatching Murray Atwood to his ancestors.

I looked for more, without getting much. She began to

fidget. She looked at her watch every other minute. She had to get home before her husband.

That sort of self-imposed deadline becomes very important to cheating spouses. The spouse with nothing to hide can be late and questions won't bring on a lingering worry that discovery has been only narrowly averted. That thought brought me to my last question, one that I wanted to phrase as delicately as I could.

"Is there anyone else who might have a strong emotional interest in you, Mrs. Devlin?"

She wasn't sure what I was driving at. That's the problem with trying to be delicate.

"Another lover," I explained, dropping my attempt at beating around the bush. "Past, present, or potential. Someone who might have looked upon Atwood as a rival, or love thief. Someone who might have been consumed, as they say, with jealousy."

"No," she said quickly. Too quickly. "Do you think that I maintain a stable of men?" Too much protest.

"I'm a detective, Mrs. Devlin. I may find out anyway, but before that happens I could cause a lot of problems for us both by stumbling around in the dark, asking the wrong questions of the wrong people."

She chewed on her lip some more. "There was someone," she admitted. "It's over now. He's out of my life."

"Name?"

She didn't want to give it to me. I pointed out that we both needed someone other than the two of us for the cops to take an interest in. Besides, did she want to shield a possible murderer, even if he was an ex-lover?

"Carlos Ramirez," she told me. It turned out that he had a longer name than that. "Juan Carlos Ramirez-Pondal," she added.

He held a top spot in a South American embassy in Washington, Counselor for Economic Affairs. She'd met him through her husband. He had swept her off her feet.

He was that kind of guy, apparently. Incredibly hand-
some, charming, and gallant. Your basic Latin lover. The
affair had lasted a year. She broke it off, believing that
someone she did not much care for had discovered the
romance and might try to use it against her.

"Did Ramirez accept being dumped? That type usually
doesn't."

"Carlos isn't any type," she said, without explaining.
She almost sounded as though she meant it.

"Whatever," I said, jotting down the details. "Who
else?"

"Damn you," she said and stood up. "No one else."
She strode angrily across the floor to the door, jerked it
open, passed through the doorway, and slammed the
door behind her.

I sighed and stood up and went around the desk. She
hadn't touched her Scotch so I drank it and cleared away
the cups and bottle. Paula Devlin's husband didn't sound
like the forgiving sort, so I couldn't blame her for being
on edge. I also couldn't blame her for worrying more
about her husband than she did about the cops. When
those letters turned up, it might cost her more than she
could afford to keep them away from Mr. Devlin.

I went back to my chair and sat down, thinking. She
hadn't given me much to start with, but what she had
given me was all I had, and I had to start using it. I
couldn't just sit around drinking Scotch and hoping that
Detective Paddock would go away and bother someone
else he liked less than he did me.

4

AN HOUR AND a half later, I walked into the rotunda of
Carlos Ramirez's embassy. At my side, holding my arm
as though it would contaminate her, was a medium-
height dishwater blonde. She had a large nose, legs too
short for the rest of her, and a manner that was all
business.

Ahead of us were three men and two women loosely
lined up to shake hands with a smiling man in a black
tuxedo and a tight-faced woman in a long, red dress. My
companion muttered to me that it was Ramirez and wife,
and we lined up behind the others.

"Wanda," said the man, showing perfect white teeth
and a dazzling smile. The whole force of the smile was
directed toward the blonde. It must have had its intended
effect. Her tentative hold on my arm tightened. I hoped
she wasn't about to swoon. "How grand of you to
come," he said.

Wanda introduced me to Ramirez as her "friend." I
guessed him to be about my age, possibly a little
younger. He had black hair, black eyes, and a black
mustache. Apparently he'd spent some time in the States
because he didn't stand nose to nose, a disconcerting
habit Latin Americans have. Disconcerting, that is, to
North Americans.

He had a smile for me, too, as did Señora Ramirez, but
her eyes watched Wanda. Ramirez's firm handshake,
with that practiced tug of the professional greeter, pro-
pelled us beyond them further into the vast room.

We joined a crowd of maybe 150, possibly 200, other people. Most of the men wore dark business suits, but here and there you could see the occasional tuxedo. There were more long dresses than tuxedoes, but most of the women wore cocktail dresses or evening pants suits. A few women wore daytime suits, having presumably come directly from the office. I was the only one in the place wearing a sport jacket. At least I had put on the office tie.

Wanda dropped my arm. "Don't make an ass of yourself," she cautioned me.

"I'm fairly confident that I won't knock over the punch bowl. I've been practicing."

She glared at me and disappeared into the crowd, obviously delighted to put distance between us. I didn't hold it against her. It had not been her idea, but she hadn't been my first choice either.

I had wanted to see Walter Devlin, but his secretary told me that he had left for the day and had not said where he was going. That left me with Juan Carlos Ramirez-Pondal. Sometimes Latin American diplomats open up late and thus close late. I hoped for a chance of catching Ramirez still in his office.

Ramirez's secretary set me straight. "I'm sorry, sir," she said. "Mr. Ramirez has left for the day." Then, apparently feeling the need to explain, she added, "The Economic Section is holding its annual Christmas party."

She didn't have to add that if I were anyone Ramirez should have known, I would have received an invitation to his party, because that's the way Washington works. Parties are for the conducting of business—commercial, diplomatic, political—not fun. Not even holiday-season parties are exempt.

"Will he be in the office tomorrow?" I asked politely. "Perhaps I could call in the morning."

"I'm sorry, sir," she answered. "He'll be in New York tomorrow. I don't expect him back until sometime Wednesday."

"It's rather important," I suggested hopefully. "Possibly you could give me his home phone number."

Her voice turned icy. "I'm sorry, sir. I cannot divulge that information." With that, she hung up.

Well, I had ways of getting Ramirez's home number but another notion wiggled its way into my mind, and it seemed a lot more fun. I play poker on Thursday nights with some guys who have more seniority in Washington than I do. One night the conversation included some tales on the nearly extinct sport of diplomatic-party gate-crashing. There was a time when a few daring spirits dedicated their every waking moments to devising new and more bizarre ways to get past the butler at the front door without an invitation. These were the dedicated ones for whom the thrill had moved from the attraction of free booze and food and mixing with the rich and famous to the challenge of the act itself.

Then the world changed. The guy who didn't belong at the party wasn't there to have fun anymore. He came to kidnap or to kill or to take hostages. It was no longer the butler at the door but hard-eyed security men, and the penalty for getting caught became a good deal stiffer than being quietly asked to leave.

So you don't hear as much about the famous crashers as you used to. It's like that's all over. The crazies with the guns and the explosives have taken a lot of the fun out of life.

I had called one of the poker players, a man high up in the Commerce Department, with my idea.

"Larry," I said. "You guys have a bureau of foreign trade, don't you?" He gave me the correct name of it. "And you'd have country desk officers who'd get invited to embassy parties, wouldn't you?" He agreed. Larry liked to think that the country desk officer in the Department of Commerce was as important to foreign embassy economic officers as the State Department desk officer was to the political officers at those embassies. He might have been right, for all I knew.

I explained what I wanted, and Larry agreed to see what he could do, which led to Wanda.

"Is this a CIA operation?" she had wanted to know when I picked her up.

"If it was, would I tell you?" I had replied.

That satisfied her that it was indeed a CIA gig and reinforced her resolve to avoid me once she got me past the two tuxedoed security types at the door. Only I wouldn't let her go until she introduced me briefly to Juan Carlos.

Now I was on my own. I doubted that I'd be seeing Wanda again unless she got an hors d'oeuvre caught in her throat and I was the only one within miles who knew the Heimlich maneuver.

Being alone and friendless in a strange place, I did the most sensible thing. I went to one of the bars. It was a bench-type arrangement covered with a snowy white tablecloth and lots of bottles and glasses. A bowl of punch sat at one end and another of eggnog at the opposite end. In between, two busy bartenders wearing white shirts, black bow ties, and suspenders dispersed a variety of other drinks. One of them gave me a Scotch and water, and I began, as the phrase goes, to circulate.

Ramirez was finishing up his greeting chores. More people were yet to arrive, but the late-comers would have to seek him out if they wanted to see him. If someone arrived whom Ramirez wanted to see, Ramirez would be told about it by one of his staff on the lookout for the VIP's.

In the meantime, I had to wait for a good opening, so I had to keep my eye on him. I drifted through the crowd avoiding any commitment to an extended conversation. Once, trapped, I simply walked away. Rude, maybe, but like most of the people there, I was on business.

A high ceiling arched over our heads, allowing the noise and tobacco smoke to rise away from the people making it. In the center of the floor stood a tall, lighted tree, around which were buffet tables loaded with turkey, ham, beef slices, and rolls to wrap around the meat. Large bowls with slices and balls of fruit alternated around the tree with plates of cheese. Large brass warmers sat at each corner containing meatballs. Where room on the tables could be found, white-jacketed waiters deposited trays of other hot hors d'oeuvres—cheese, pâté, or clam filling in the center of fluffy pastry wrappings—slipping out the empty trays and replacing them with full ones. Other waiters moved through the crowd with smaller trays of the hors d'oeuvres, tempting those whose conversations had grown too interesting to leave for food.

There are people in Ramirez's country who don't get enough to eat, but you weren't supposed to think about those things at embassy parties. It makes the guests uncomfortable. Besides, the problem isn't that there is too little food, it's the money to buy it that is lacking. That's why we pay the world's best farmers not to grow food while people starve in Africa.

My starving wasn't going to help them any, and my stomach had begun reminding me of how long it had been since lunch. I was glad Ramirez had moved closer to the food, so that I could make myself a small ham sandwich. I demolished it in sacrifice to the ominous growls in my midsection.

"They are just too delicious," said a female voice at my elbow. "And that tree. Isn't it beautiful?"

I agreed as best I could with my mouth full of ham and roll, as I turned toward her. She was mid-thirties and wore a simple black dress which crossed in front to form a V down to her cleavage, which wasn't bad. She also wore engagement and wedding rings on her left hand.

"Carlos does know how to give a party," she went on.

"You know him well?" I asked.

She snatched up one of the clam pastries with a dainty and practiced movement. "Uh-huh," she said, swallowing and chasing it down with a sip of white wine from the glass she carried in the hand with the rings. "From ages ago. We were stationed in Caracas at the same time." Another hors d'oeuvre disappeared into her lush, red mouth. "I shouldn't eat another one of these. My God, my figure is going to hell. I'll have to fast for a month."

I didn't think so, and I told her. "Don't change a thing," I said. She filled out the black dress amply, but not excessively, in all the right places.

"You're not government," she said, looking me over with an eye which told me that she could tell.

"Huh-uh," I replied. "Private business." I pointed to her wine glass. "Can I get you a refill?"

"That would be nice. Thank you."

She followed me to the bar and stood on the fringes of the thirsting patrons while I plunged through and got our glasses refilled. "Thanks," she said. "I'm Stephanie."

"I'm Dan," I said.

She peered through the crowd. "That's Frank over there," she said, with a slight inclination of her head. "He hates it when I tag around after him at these things."

Frank glanced over toward us. He was a short, corpulent man with a red, intense face and suspicious eyes. He gave us the full benefit of that suspicion. Stephanie wiggled her fingers toward him in greeting. He looked away, annoyed.

"He thinks I should find some other wives whose husbands might be important to him and make girl talk. He's probably right, but I don't like talking to women. I like men."

32

She looked in the direction of Ramirez, standing a little away from the buffet table. I had been watching him, and I wondered if she had noticed. If she had, she gave no indication, only a little sigh.

"Carlos is a devil," she said, "but so beautiful. Give him half an hour alone with any woman in this room, and he would have her in bed."

"Any woman in this room?"

She looked back to me, her eyes twinkling mischievously. "Nearly any," she said. "Women drool over Carlos."

"Some guys have all the luck."

She looked at me with lustrous eyes. "I'd guess that you have your share," she said. "Unfortunately for me, I'm stuck with old chubbs over there. All I can do is stand back and envy the girls with more nerve than I have. When it comes to amorous adventures, I'm chicken." She smiled coyly. "Enjoy yourself, Dan. It's a nice party to crash. You make a lousy businessman."

She moved off in the direction of a knot of men involved in an earnest discussion. I watched her go, conscious of appetites a ham sandwich wouldn't do anything for. I tugged my glance away and sent it in search of our host.

He had moved farther away from the huge table. I moved in his direction. Three adoring women surrounded him. Beyond, Maria Ramirez, her red dress a seeming danger signal, kept her eye on him, and he obviously knew it. My moment looked as though it had arrived.

I ambled over to Ramirez, who pretended that he was glad to see me. "Ah, my friend," he said effusively. "You are holding me to my promise to get down to business." He apologized to his fans and steered me away with a hand behind my elbow, not an easy thing to do with a man five inches taller and fifty pounds heavier than you. Still he managed.

"Thanks, pal," he said in perfect colloquial English. His words told me he knew the women to whom he had been talking. You don't say things like that to a stranger unless you are sure he's not married to one of the people who has been boring you. "Sorry to put you on the spot, but I needed help."

"You didn't seem to be hurting," I said.

"One of those women is married to a man who will decide whether to put a major auto-parts factory either in my country or in Brazil," he said. "You think I want her husband to see her climbing all over me?"

"How can you help yourself?"

He looked at me warily and then broke into a laugh. "What did you say your name was?" he asked, showing me his star-quality teeth.

"Cronyn," I replied.

"Cronyn, huh," he repeated, thinking. "Yes. You came with Wanda . . . , he hesitated but only briefly, "Guzman." He considered me with amused eyes. "Not your type. Not your type at all."

"So she told me. I conned her into bringing me."

His eyes didn't lose any of their amusement. "Looking for a free happy hour?"

"No. Looking for you. I wasn't having much luck with your secretary."

"Okay. So now you've found me. Enjoy the party." He started to move away.

I spoke to his back. "I saw Paula Devlin today."

His shoulders stiffened. He turned back slowly to face me. "Who did you say?" His voice was polite, his eyes cautious.

"Paula Devlin. You do know her, don't you?"

"Slightly. I . . ." A waiter arrived with a tray of drinks. Ramirez took one while saying hello to another guest. He turned to me. "Let's go where we can talk more privately."

34

I nodded and followed him through a door into a short hall. From there we entered a small room with tall bookcases, a spacious desk, and two leather easy chairs. Only two small lamps illuminated the room.

Ramirez eased himself into one of the chairs and dropped one leg over its arm. "What about Paula Devlin?" he asked me.

"When did you last see her?"

"Last Friday evening. I stopped by the place in Georgetown to have a drink with her husband. Our paths crossed in the hall. Why?"

"She's in some trouble."

He looked genuinely concerned. "What kind of trouble?"

"She wrote some letters. She wants them back. She asked me to help get them. Do you have them?"

The concern on his face turned to bafflement. "Letters? What letters? I don't know anything about any letters." The bafflement seemed as genuine as the concern.

"Ever hear of a man named Murray Atwood?"

"No. Never. What the hell is going on, Cronyn? Who is Atwood?"

"He used to be a blackmailer. Somebody put him out of business today with six slugs from a thirty-two caliber revolver."

"What's that got to do with me?"

"This. Any of the adult population of Washington, D.C., and its environs could have shot Atwood, which gives the cops a lot to work with. But I'm only interested in getting the letters, so I'm starting with those people who might have had a reason for wanting to help Paula Devlin out of a jam."

He examined his fingernails. "What did Paula tell you about me?"

"That you two had been getting it off together."

"Jesus, Cronyn!" He looked up quickly, throwing a sharp glance toward the door and straightening in his chair.

I looked at the door, too. It was thick and solid and securely shut. "Well?" I said, looking back to him. "The lady seems to be quite truthful in the matter."

He relaxed into the chair once more. A smile lifted the corners of his mustache. "I'll bet she didn't put it quite the way you did?"

"No," I said. "In fact, she didn't want to put it at all. She said that you were out of her life. She didn't say you were a friend of her husband's."

"I'm not. Occasionally Walter has a client who expresses an interest in overseas investment. My country seeks American investment. Thus it is to our mutual advantage to talk."

"She said that it was over between you two. Is it?"

His black eyes looked directly into mine. "Yes. She ended it because she was afraid that she'd been caught."

"You don't sound too happy about it."

He didn't give me a response right away. He looked away, toward the door. "I don't make a habit of becoming involved with married women," he said. "Paula was different. She seemed so . . . unapproachable is the word, I guess."

"A challenge."

He gave me a small smile. "I suppose. Who knows why one particular woman fascinates one particular man?"

"If you did and could bottle it, your fortune would be made. Tell me about this fascination. Does it still exist?"

He shook his head slowly. "Nope," he replied. "I wouldn't want to see the lady hurt, you understand, especially by something that I had contributed to, but that's as far as it goes."

He seemed sincere, but I reminded myself that he was

a diplomat. He was supposed to be able to pat you on the back while he picked your pocket.

"It doesn't go as far as shooting her new lover?"

"I wouldn't shoot anybody," he said, smiling again. "She had another man in her life, did she? Well, that surprises me."

"After you, she was spoiled for anything but the very best, you mean."

A flash of anger crossed his face, stayed there momentarily, and left, pushed away by an engaging grin. "You must make a lot of friends, Cronyn."

"I'm not in the business of making friends."

"You're in the business of returning letters to married women. Private investigator?"

"That's right."

"I can't help you. I wish I could, since Paula seems to have something at stake in this. You say she wrote the letters, and somehow this man Atwood came into possession of them, and that he was a blackmailer. And now the letters are missing. Do you know what was in those letters?"

"In general, yes."

"But you aren't saying," Ramirez suggested.

"You're right. I'm not."

"Can you tell me if there was anything in those letters concerning me?"

I took my time answering him, because his question seemed out of step with what I had already told him. Nothing in that should have given him reason to think Paula Devlin had confessed to her love affair with Ramirez in those letters. On the contrary, the most likely inference he could have drawn was the correct one, that Paula Devlin had written indiscreet intimacies to her new lover. That possibility never seemed to occur to him.

"No," I said, confidently. She had not told me, but the last thing a woman is likely to include in her letters of passion to her lover would be any references to the guy who preceded him. "Those letters did not mention you."

"Just wanted to be sure," he said. He looked at his watch. "Back to the trenches," he added and stood out of the chair.

"Mind telling me where you were this afternoon, say from twelve to three?"

"Part of the time I was on an airplane and part of the time on my way home from Dulles Airport in a taxicab. I spent the weekend in my home country."

"The cab wouldn't have come past Observatory Circle, would it?"

"Could hardly have avoided it," Ramirez replied. "I stopped at the embassy on my way, and I live just off Cathedral Avenue. Why?"

"Atwood lived at a place west of Wisconsin Avenue. I drove out to his place today. I went out Mass, around Observatory Circle, and across Wisconsin to get there. It seems we were both in Atwood's neighborhood."

"So it seems," He smiled again. "I really must return to my party, Mr. Cronyn."

I slid my butt off the desk. "Thanks for your time, Mr. Ramirez. If you can think of anything else, give me a call." I handed him one of my business cards.

Behind me the door opened, to the accompaniment of angry words in Spanish. I turned. Mrs. Ramirez stepped into the room, saw me, and halted, confused. Her eyes went from me to Ramirez, then around the room as if not believing only the two of us were in the room. She stood there in an embarrassed silence.

Ramirez came to her rescue. "My dear," he said. "You remember Mr. Cronyn. We needed a few minutes of privacy for business, but you're quite right to remind me that we have other guests." He looked at me, a small, genuine smile playing around the corners of his mouth. "Shall we, Mr. Cronyn?"

We returned to the party. Ramirez joined a knot of men conversing seriously and gave them something they could chuckle over. I saw nothing of Wanda or Stephanie, so I left the party, thinking that a man can be too damned successful with women for his own good, especially a man who already has a wife.

5

I RETRIEVED MY coat from the woman tending coats and hats. I crossed the marble floor of the large foyer heading for the outside door and the cold wind blowing along Mass Avenue. I stopped halfway to the door.

A small anteroom lay to my left, its door partially open. A man sat in the room. Through the partially opened door I could see only a shoulder, an elbow propped on the arm of a nice chair, and a hand holding a newspaper. On the table beside him lay a hat. It was the hat that caught my attention. It was one of those soft, plaid, brimmed jobs with a little red feather stuck in the band. It looked familiar.

I shrugged, started for the door again, and stopped again, halted by my curiosity. I told myself, "What the hell," and went back and entered the room, closing the door behind me silently.

I walked up to the man in the chair and spoke to the newspaper. "Working, Pappy?" I asked politely. "Or are you lost?"

The newspaper twitched and, after half an instant, began a slow descent, revealing first slicked-down gray hair, then salt-and-pepper eyebrows, followed by a face featuring a bulbous nose and taut lips.

"Don't be a wiseass," he grated out. He looked toward the door and then back to me. He didn't look glad to see me.

"Anybody know that you're out here?" I asked him.

Pappy growled at me without saying anything intelligible. He folded up the paper and stuck it down into the chair. "I've got a job," he replied.

"Here?" I said, unable to hide my disbelief.

"No, you dumb bastard. The job's in Foggy Bottom. I'm just here getting warm."

I ignored his attempt at sarcasm. "What's the deal, Pappy?" He didn't want to tell me. I asked again and added, "I'm looking for something, Pappy. I came here thinking I might find out where I might find that something. I didn't, and I'd like to know if maybe somebody here hired you to find, or obtain, the same thing."

He looked at me with blank eyes. "What the hell are you talking about?"

"Letters."

He shook his head. "Don't know anything about any letters."

"Who are you working for, Pappy? Carlos Ramirez?"

The blank look left his eyes to be replaced by an uncertain wariness. He pressed his lips together in stubborn silence.

"Okay," I said, "I'll go back and ask Ramirez."

"For crissakes, Cronyn," he growled. "It's worth twenty if you keep your mouth shut," he offered.

Pappy didn't get many jobs anymore, so he needed his twenty more than I did. "Put it toward your retirement," I said. "I'm open to an even trade. I won't say anything to Ramirez if you tell me what the job is."

Suspicion turned the corners of his mouth down. "There's only enough action here for one guy," he warned.

"I'm not trying to crowd in," I assured him. "I've got more than I can handle. I just want to know what the job is."

Pappy tried to argue the ethics of the situation, which with Pappy was a little like a duck trying on trousers, but I had to give him credit for making the effort. Then I leaned on him some more.

42

"If that's the way you want it," I said and turned toward the door.

"All right," he said to my back. "All the damned right."

He took a deep breath. "Ramirez's old lady," he said. "I'm on a job for her." He thought that much would satisfy me. When he saw that it wouldn't, he said, "Jeez, Cronyn, gimme a break. She thinks he's playing around. You see, he takes trips back home every month or so."

"To South America?"

"Yeah. The señora thinks that he's got a hot tamale stashed down there and another one here. I guess she can't do anything about the one down there but I'm supposed to find out who it is he's playing around with here."

"He sounds like a busy man."

"He's a dago, ain't he? They're all like that. Can't keep their hands off women, and some women go for guys like that."

"Anybody in particular?"

He took time to think over whether he should answer or not. Finally he heaved his tired-looking shoulders and said, "Nothing steady, not that I can see, anyway."

"How long have you been on him?"

"On and off since last Thursday, whenever the old lady gets suspicious," he replied. "Like today. He's coming back from one of his trips. The señora thinks he ought to get home sooner than he does from the airport. I guess she figures he gets something on the way from Dulles. Anyway, she had me stake him out there."

"After he's spent the weekend with his mistress in South America?" I asked. "You don't suppose he'd be too tired, I mean, after all that activity back home?"

"You don't know those dagos the way I do, Cronyn. They never get tired screwing. It's because they're raised in all that hot weather, I think. It does something to their glands."

I wasn't sure Pappy was used to thinking, but I stayed silent on the matter. A small, smug smile spread over his face. He couldn't wait to tell me what caused it.

"Fancy pants headed straight from the airport to a massage parlor in D.C. to get his rocks off. See what I mean? It's all they think about. That's why those crap countries down there never amount to anything. They wear themselves out screwing and don't have enough energy left to do any work, so we gotta support them."

"Are you putting me on, Pappy?"

He looked offended. "Why the hell should I do that?"

Why indeed, I thought, as I considered what he had told me. "Which massage parlor?" I asked.

"The Just Heavenly. It's on 14th."

"You stayed with him?"

He hesitated before replying. "Couldn't," he said. "I had to go up after him, you know." I knew. Pappy had to go into the building to find out which of the several businesses Ramirez might have visited. You can't do that sitting in a car on the street outside.

"Sonofabitch doubled back on me sooner than I expected. Met me on the stairs. Wasn't anything I could do but break it off."

"Tough luck," I commiserated with him. "How long was he up there?"

"About ten minutes."

"Ten minutes?"

"You've heard about Speedy Gonzales, haven't you?" Pappy smirked, sure in his prejudices.

"What time was that?"

"Two-twenty."

I had arrived at Atwood's apartment at three-fifteen. He'd been a corpse for about an hour was the first guess. It could have been something less than that or something more. The window of opportunity could have allowed Ramirez time to take care of Atwood. And if he had not done the shooting, that same window could have allowed him to beat me to the apartment and lift the letters.

I gave Pappy MacClearn an appraising look. "He saw you today," I said. "It's a little risky coming here to-night, isn't it?"

Pappy shrugged. "He saw me good, too good. Job's over."

"Are you recommending another man to her?"

Pappy's glance slid downward to about the level of the knot in my tie. "I get just enough work to pay the rent," he said. "I hoped this job would last, on and off, a couple of weeks, at least." He paused. "All she owes me is four hundred." Another pause. "I need the money, Cronyn."

You don't like to think it happens in this business, but it does. "How much do you think you'll get from him?"

"I told him to have two grand in cash," replied Pappy. "If he doesn't think it's worth that much, I'll take one."

"And for that you'll tell Mrs. Ramirez her husband is clean," I said, "and that she's wasting her money having him followed."

Pappy didn't answer me, and he didn't look me in the eye. I buttoned my coat and turned up my collar. "Forget this chat," I ordered him.

Pappy nodded. He would forget. He wouldn't get much from Ramirez if Ramirez found out someone else knew about the visit to the Just Heavenly. Pappy would have to assure him that the information died when the money passed.

I turned and went out to the cold.

I tell myself that I shouldn't form quick opinions about people I meet in the course of pursuing my line of work. Sometimes it turns out all right. Other times the people we think we know turn out entirely different from what we have led ourselves to expect. It's not that people fool us, it's that we fool ourselves. We meet someone and get a surface picture of them and then we subconsciously start filling in the gaps of that picture with pieces of experience from our own backgrounds. Then the person acts in a way we don't expect, and we often resent it.

Still, I go on, occasionally at least, forming opinions about people from first impressions, which is how I wound up parked across the street from the Just Heavenly massage parlor. The opinion I had formed concerned Carlos Ramirez, and it clashed with the idea that Ramirez would pump six bullets into a man sitting on a couch wearing his slippers, drinking a leisurely Scotch, and smoking a cigar.

It also clashed with the notion of him needing to visit a massage parlor to satisfy his physical needs. All the evidence pointed to the guy having too many willing women, not too few. The elegant, debonair Carlos sleazing out? This, only hours after leaving his mistress in South America?

Soon after leaving Ramirez's embassy, I found a telephone and consulted the Yellow Pages. The Just Heavenly massage parlor had the smallest ad the telephone company will sell you. The ad gave only the name of the place, the address, and the phone number "for outcall service." The ad made no attempt to promote the services offered by the establishment, from which you might conclude that it had an already sufficient clientele and did not wish to spend money on advertising, or that it was very exclusive, or anything.

I slid out of the station wagon, locked the door, and crossed the street to the address in the phone book. It was a doorway with steps leading to the second and third floors of an old red-brick building. On one side of the doorway was the entrance to a topless and bottomless go-go bar. On the other side, with windows painted yellow to the height of a tall man, was an adult bookshop, which also advertised itself as an outlet for sex aids, the sorts of things that some men think women are just dying to have stuck in them.

I climbed the stairs to the third floor, passing, at the second, the glassed-in front of the Emperor of China Delights massage parlor. The glass allowed a tantalizing glimpse of almond-eyed young women in gauzy see-thru blouses.

Just Heavenly, on the third floor, had no such come-on. A small sign on a black door told me I had arrived at the right place. I opened the door and went in. An enormously fat black woman who looked to be about fifty sat behind a desk that looked like it had come from the same government-surplus sale as mine. A black guy wearing a white sweater and black trousers sat on a wooden bench leafing through a comic book.

He looked up at me but didn't say anything. I crossed the bare wooden floor, noticing that it needed to be swept, to the desk. The walls of the room could have used a paint job. I supposed the photos of naked women kept most of the customers distracted.

The woman, wearing a bright caftan that could have covered Barnum & Bailey's main tent, looked up. "Yeah?" she asked.

Since there was nothing in the ad to attract a customer to this place, and since I doubted a walk-in from the street would pass up the promise of the Emperor of China, I had to give another reason for being there.

"A guy I know recommended the place," I said. "Thought I'd check it out." Which was about as far as I planned to go. She saved me explaining why I wasn't interested in immediate service.

"What you see is what you get," she said. "It's early. Not all the ladies are here yet. Those that are, are on call. You wanta go back and strip?" She waved an arm vaguely in the direction of a door behind her.

"I was figuring on somebody a little younger," I said.

It didn't bother her. Business is business. You can't take it personally.

"Try the gooks downstairs," she said. "They spell relief crossways." She chuckled. Mounds of flesh rolled under the cloth of her garment.

The black guy got up. He was about my age and about three inches shorter. He was skinny. I figured he carried a knife somewhere, but I couldn't figure out where.

He came over to me and looked at me, his eyes squinting up for a good look. "I seen you somewhere," he said. His eyes meshed with his memory and clicked with recognition. "He's some kind of private cop," he told the fat woman. His eyes glowed yellowly.

The woman looked up. "You sure?" she asked.

"Yeah. He repossessed Little Purple Washington's car once," he replied. "Little Purple had this Chrysler, see. Don't know how he come to get a damned Chrysler, not having any money, see. He never make a payment, not one damned payment, Jacquie," he went on, addressing the woman. "Hey, the bank wanted that car back so bad they pissed all over Anacostia. But Little Purple kept moving it around, so's they couldn't get it, 'till this dude comes along."

The woman called Jacquie looked up at me. I shrugged. I knew the end of the story.

"Little Purple liked to show off at a restaurant uptown, a white place. He flashing a big car and a white woman, see. Big shot. He drives up, and the honky parking the cars comes out. Little Purple says, 'Hey boy, give it a shine,' laughs like hell, and takes his woman in the restaurant. Honky gets in the car, drives toward the parking lot, and Little Purple never sees his car again." He laughed heartily. His eyes continued to glow yellowly.

Jacquie said to me, "You?"

I sighed. "Yeah," I replied.

"What do you want around here?" she asked.

"Like I said. A friend of mine has been here. I was checking it out. It's personal."

"Has this friend got a name?"

"Yeah, but I doubt he'd use it here."

"How about you? What do they call you?"

"Cronyn."

"Well, Cronyn. I run a legitimate business. Clean, honest girls. It doesn't look like much here, but most of my business is outcall." She picked up a book. "You want a massage tonight or not? That's all my girls sell. If you're looking to get fucked, go somewhere else. If you're just looking, get lost."

"A man by the name of Murray Atwood was shot today."

The mention of the name seemed to make no impression on her. "It happens."

"He had something belonging to a client of mine, before he was killed. Now nobody seems able to find it."

"That's too bad. Was this something valuable?"

"To my client."

She shrugged. "I hope you find it then. What's it got to do with me?"

"One of your customers might have had an interest in getting hold of this material, for personal reasons. He doesn't seem to be the type to go around shooting people, but he might have asked in certain circles how to get some help. Not to shoot Atwood but to persuade him. I don't care who shot him, just who took off with my client's material."

"Like I said earlier, Cronyn, I run a legitimate business."

"You might know of someone."

"I know a lot of people, but I stay away from people who make their living with guns."

"My client was willing to pay ten thousand to Atwood

to get the material back. If you have it, I might be able to arrange the same deal."

"What kind of material is it?" she asked.

"If you had it, I guess you'd know what it was."

"That's the way I look at it, too," she replied. "Who is the customer?"

"It doesn't make any difference, as long as he didn't have you do anything for him."

"Maybe he talked to one of my girls," she said. "We do an outcall business."

I took out a card and put it on her desk. "If the idea of making ten thou sharpens anyone's memory, give me a call."

"Don't hold your breath," the huge black woman told me.

"I won't."

I walked to the door. The skinny guy in the white sweater came with me. We went down the steps together to the sidewalk. He lit a cigarette and sucked in the smoke.

"Germaine, isn't it? Jacquie, I mean," I said.

"Yeah, man. You remember her?" he said. His voice held surprise.

"Little Purple used to work for her some," I said. "The story of his car and you calling her Jacquie brought it back. Jacquie Germaine, Queen of the Number."

"Hey, man, you got a good memory. That was a long time ago."

"Before the government started its own lottery," I said. "I heard she was dead."

"Naw. Just sick. And broke. She's doing okay now. She seen Jesus and everything," he said, winking and walking away in a cloud of tobacco smoke, leaving me to ponder the question I had started with.

Why had Ramirez visited a sleazy massage parlor directly from Dulles Airport?

6

DETECTIVE PADDOCK CAME to see me the next day.

I walked through the door to my office after a late Tuesday lunch and found him sitting behind my desk, in my chair, still wearing his raincoat. He had searched the desk. The address book where I recorded the name of Pamela Davidson and her phony address lay open before him, at the D's.

"I don't remember handing out keys," I said.

He grunted. "The building guy downstairs. Very cooperative."

"Ralph sweats a lot at the sight of a badge." Ralph also tended the little room downstairs where the master keys for the building are located.

Paddock's finger tapped the address book, and he said, "Pamela Davidson. Yeah." His eyes focused on mine. "Old couple, name of Lefcowitz, live at that address. Never heard of Pamela Davidson. Surprise, surprise."

I sat down in the same chair Paula Devlin had used the day before. I had used up a sunny and mild winter morning learning nothing about Murray Atwood from the credit bureau, the phone company, and the rental office at Northwest Gardens. All that came after Devlin's secretary told me he was out of town, participating in several businessmen's seminars in the Midwest. It didn't help my outlook on life to come back to the office and find Paddock sitting in my chair.

I waved my hand at the desk. "Didn't I read something

somewhere about you needing a search warrant for that? I'm almost sure I did."

He laughed a short, mirthless laugh. He closed the address book and replaced it in the upper right-hand drawer. He leaned back in the chair.

"Why don't you tell me why you killed Murray Atwood?" he asked. "Once that's done, we can be friends."

"You have my story."

"You're going to stick with that?" he asked. "Big mistake, cowboy. I'm going to have your ass if you don't do better than that."

What he wanted, of course, was for me to start changing my story. Revisions, embellishments. Add a little here and a little there until you can't remember the first story you told.

Paddock would remember, though, and he'd compare all of the differences and zero in on them. Not just once, but everyday, twice a day, if necessary, until he had me, floundering and unable to recall all the lies I had told. You either confess when you reach that stage, or you shut up altogether, too late.

I decided that it was best just to stick to the truth. "I went there to make a deal for those letters," I said.

"Okay," he said without rancor. "Let's start with the letters. You have them?"

"No. If I did, you'd get them."

"I'd better. They're evidence in a murder investigation."

"I don't know where they are."

"You're sure?"

"I'm sure."

"Uh-huh. You looked for them, didn't you?"

I hesitated between the rock of admitting that I had looked the premises over before calling the cops as opposed to the hard place of his certain suspicion that if I had not looked it was because I knew no letters existed.

"All right," I said. "I gave the place a quick look. I didn't disturb anything."

My looking didn't seem to bother him. His face almost relaxed. "That's better," he said. "When we got there, no letters. You didn't have them, and you had not had time to get rid of them. So how'd you do it? Was the woman with you, waiting outside? You could have taken the letters to her, and she could have taken off."

"I haven't seen the letters." I told him. "Look, the door was open when I got there. He'd been dead an hour or maybe two. Who knows how many people could have come and gone during that time?"

"Just like Union Station, eh?" Paddock leaned forward and put his forearms on the desk. "You got yourself a real problem, cowboy. I guess you're just too stupid to see it. You give me a story about letters that don't exist and about a woman nobody's heard of, and you expect me to believe that."

"That's the way it happened," I said.

He laughed coldly. "I'm going to have your ass, cowboy," he said, leaning back in the chair once more. "Concealment or destruction of evidence."

"Why the hell would I destroy those letters? It wasn't me that Atwood was blackmailing."

"You had a client, right?" he asked. He didn't wait for my answer. "She was willing to pay Atwood ten thou for the letters. Maybe you figured that you could get something from her for getting rid of them. What's your price, cowboy? A quarter?"

I kept my mouth shut. I had already said enough. Paddock wanted to keep my mouth running, hoping I'd say something he could use to squeeze those letters out of me. He seemed convinced that I had them. Nothing I could say seemed likely to change his mind. More talk would only make it worse.

His mouth worked silently. His eyes roamed the room and came back to me. "You're supposed to be okay, according to a couple of people we checked with this morning," he said. "That counts in your favor."

"Thanks."

"I don't like it when you are a smart-ass."

"I'm worried."

"Now you talk like an uptown smart-ass. That's the worst kind."

"You have my story, Paddock. If I find those letters, you'll be the first to know. Now, whether you mind or not, I've got a business to run."

He didn't budge. "Ever see the victim before yesterday?"

"Atwood? No. I've never seen him, and I've never heard of him."

"We got a quick read on his prints."

"So?"

"Atwood is an alias. His real name is Theodore Francis Fromann. Ring a bell?"

"No. Should it?"

"Maybe. The FBI has an old fugitive warrant out on him," Paddock replied. "Seems that he got mixed up with some of those real bad-ass radicals. Thought you might have run across him in the old days."

I turned the name of Fromann over in my mind and searched my memory. It had been a long time ago. Some of the names were fading from my consciousness, even those of the people I'd promised to bleed with.

"I started drifting away from the movement in seventy and seventy-one," I said. "I was one of those who started questioning some of the things being done in the name of peace and justice. And some of our comrades started questioning the loyalty of those of us who asked the questions."

"Once a Commie, always a Commie," observed Paddock.

I shrugged. It didn't make any difference what Paddock thought about my politics, past or present. All that seemed like a lifetime ago. I guess it was.

"I don't know Fromann," I said. "I can't recall ever hearing the name."

Paddock stood up and headed for the door. He turned. "We can dig deep," he said.

"I go my own way now, Paddock," I told him. "I've stopped trying to change the world, and I've stopped listening to those who have all the answers, because I've found out that the questions change from election to election, depending on who's in and who's out. There isn't any peace and there's damned little justice in this world, but when I can help somebody get a little bit of one or the other, I do what I can. I guess that's why I'm in the business I'm in."

"You won't be in business much longer," he said, "if I don't see those letters. Next time I see you, cowboy, have them for me."

He went out the door, leaving it open. I went to it and closed it, then returned to my chair, sat down, and stared up at a spot on the ceiling. Fromann. Ted Fromann. The name meant nothing to me. If I'd ever heard it, I'd forgotten long ago. I had no more luck with trying to recall a face than a name. Too many years had passed. There had been too many faces, all vital with life. Fromann's was a dead face, muscles slack, eyes staring into eternity.

I supposed that he once had a vision of better things, a vision ground out of him by the need to survive. In the beginning there'd been a dream and then had come the sacrifice and the years of running.

The dream must have faded, replaced by cynicism.

One could only guess at the sense of betrayal he must have felt. A life wasted, and for what? The country had changed. The Left no longer wants to blow up the government; they embrace it. Getting rid of capitalism is out, balancing the budget is in. Tax reform replaces social reform, and everybody wants his share of the pie first.

Fromann, too, and he tried to get it in the only way he could, by squeezing the wife of a well-to-do man.

None of which meant anything. Fromann was dead, and I had to find Paula Devlin's letters, before Paddock came back.

I searched the Rolodex for some old phone numbers. It took me a while on the phone after I had compiled a list of numbers. Some were out of service, some didn't answer and those that did couldn't help, until finally I tracked down the guy I wanted, the guy who I thought could help me.

I had time to spare, so I leaned back in the chair and checked out that spot on the ceiling again. I had little use for Murray Atwood, money-grubbing blackmailer. As Ted Fromann, ex-radical, however, I could understand him—a little—and with that understanding went compassion. Yet the crime remained the same. It made Fromann no less guilty than Atwood.

So why was I looking for the reason behind Fromann's actions when I had not for Atwood? I didn't want that question. It arrived, unsummoned, the way the ones do which concern the self, the ones we try to avoid asking because we don't like the answers.

Fromann was one of "us," therefore there had to be an explanation for his crime. When one of us does something, no matter how uneasy it makes us feel, there has to be a reason, maybe a dozen reasons, behind it.

If one of "them" does the same thing, you don't look

for reasons. You don't even care if there are reasons. You denounce, or you condemn, or you punish. We don't see the individual behind the caricature. We have to look too hard to see, or listen too hard to hear, the human agony behind the label.

I gave up contemplating the ceiling. I perferred my moral armor to shine brightly, but these periodic and unwanted inspections always managed to turn up some rusty spots. Since it's the only armor I'll get, however, it'll have to do. You pay attention to the rusty places and do what can be done about them and get up and get going.

I got up and went.

I knew I'd made a mistake in agreeing to meet Charlie Hodes in Alexandria when I turned into afternoon traffic inching toward the Potomac bridges. Things picked up a little as I crossed the southbound span connecting 14th Street with Shirley Highway.

I stayed far left, slowed down through the canyon of highrises that is Crystal City, and crawled along Jeff Davis Highway until I saw the place where I was to meet Charlie. I pulled into a small parking lot that was half full, found a slot, and cut the wagon's engine. I stood out of the car and heard noises from across the highway that sounded like huge bowling balls rolling downhill. The sound puzzled me for a moment until I discovered that the restaurant stood just across the highway from a large railroad yard.

We were within the boundaries of Alexandria, I supposed, but not the part of Alexandria most people go looking for. This was not Old Town with its tiny two-centuries-old houses that sell for as much as small motels do in some parts of the country. Nor was it West Alexandria with its towering condos, nor Seminary Ridge with graceful homes and manicured lawns. This was the Alexandria of railroad yards and welding shops and used auto-parts outlets.

Charlie Hodes met me just inside the door. I had not seen him for a dozen years, but guys like Charlie are hard to forget. He was tall and had a pale, lumpy face that spoke of a bad case of teenage acne. Charlie had put on some weight since I had last seen him. He'd also lost some hair; what was left remained the same, the color of coffee with too much milk in it. Charlie always looked as though he needed a haircut but that's because he never let it grow long. He always looked like a marine recruit who hadn't seen the barber for several months, scragglylike.

Charlie looked at me intently. He looked at everyone intently. He squeezed my hand hard. That hadn't changed either.

"You buying?" he asked.

The French have a saying about how things change without changing at all. Come to think of it, the French may have more sayings than the Greeks. But you have to understand Charlie Hodes. One thing he was not was a sponger. It's just that Charlie never had any money. He abhorred money. To Charlie, money was akin to herpes. Once you had it, it changed your life and you could never get rid of it.

"I'm buying," I assured him, and we went to a table in a crowded little area off to the left of the entrance. It was the lounge and it was doing a good business. Charlie had saved us a booth. Don't ask me how. I could never figure out how Charlie got the things done that he did anymore than I could figure out how he lived without money.

"Gotta show you this, Cronyn," he said as we sat down. So far not a word about the dozen years since I'd last seen him.

He ordered Scotch, and I ordered a Manhattan. The

58

drinks arrived, as Charlie pointed out gleefully, in a little toy train that ran around two walls of the lounge from the bar, serving a half-dozen booths. It rattled its little self around the toy tracks, a little headlight shining from its toy engine. It stopped at our booth. Charlie lifted our drinks from one of the freight cars, and the train proceeded to back up, all the way back to the bar.

"The Potomac yards are just across the street," said a happy Charlie, explaining the obvious.

We sipped our drinks, and Charlie turned serious. "Never see you around anymore, Cronyn," he said accusingly. That was one way of covering twelve years in a hurry.

"My feet wore out, Charlie," I told him. "And we weren't getting anywhere. Just from one public building to another."

Charlie shook his head. "You can't give up, man," he said. "Not now, when there's new vitality, a whole new generation discovering what we knew years ago."

"Good. I hope they all go to work and pay into Social Security so it doesn't go broke when I need it."

Charlie cocked his head at me and waggled a finger. "Cynicism," he said. "That's what it is. It's the age, the Age of Cynicism. It destroyed it all for us. Everybody went their own way. Selfish cynicism. I never thought it would happen to you, Cronyn. Never. You had ideals, man. We looked up to you."

"Cynics are made out of romantics who lost their ideals, Charlie," I replied.

"Who said that?" he wanted to know.

"Charlie," I said, ignoring the question, "Fromann. Ted Fromann. Go back, Charlie. Fifteen years, maybe more. Who was Ted Fromann? Where was he coming from?"

Charlie pursed his lips, thinking, lining up all the binary channels in his brain. He finished his drink. I ordered another round, and they came on the little toy train.

"Where?" he asked. "Chicago? Berkeley? Gimme a place, a happening." Charlie tended to think in terms of events, not of years.

I shook my head. "I don't know," I admitted. "Try the Weathermen."

A scowl darkened Charlie's brow. "I wasn't into that," he said. "Too heavy."

"Come on, Charlie," I pleaded. "Think. You knew some of them, before they formed the Weathermen."

"That's going way back, Cronyn."

Suddenly Charlie looked very tired and older than he had earlier. "It's hard to remember," he said, without looking up. "Too many years. Too many people come and gone."

I let a minute pass before I spoke again. "Who do I go to, Charlie?"

He looked up. "Why muck around in the past?" he asked.

"I want to know who Fromann was," I said.

"Was?"

"Somebody put six bullets into him. I found the body. He was living under an assumed name. The Feds had a fugitive warrant out on him," I explained.

"You working for the police now?" he asked, his eyes full of suspicion.

"No," I told him. "I'm a private investigator."

"So I heard. Like it?"

"It's a living," I replied, thinking that I should have been out looking for a paying client instead of raking up a long ago past while sitting in a bar where the drinks were served by a toy train. I began to wonder if that's what happens to you when you turn forty and wonder where it's all gone.

"Got any grass?" asked Charlie.

"No. Will it help you remember if I get some?"

He shook his head. "Forget it," he said. "Forget Fromann."

"Names, Charlie, goddamnit. People who might have known Fromann." I had my notebook out.

"Not too many of that crowd around here," Charlie explained, "at least not that I know of. I can give you some names in California, and I know a couple of people in Oregon."

"No good, Charlie. Whoever wasted Fromann didn't come all the way from Oregon to do it. I also want to know what Fromann was doing here, besides blackmailing his girlfriend."

"Blackmail?" Charlie repeated. He wore a blank look on his face. "One of our people?"

"That's right. He'd been romancing a married woman. She wrote him letters, the kind in which intimate moments are relived. I want to know who else might have known about those letters or about the affair."

Charlie nodded his head. He was hurt. You could see that. Charlie lived in a world where the good guys all wore white hats and were expected to keep them spotless.

"He'd been on the run for years, Charlie. Neither you nor I know what that's like, what it can do to you. Maybe it grinds you down to where nothing matters but survival. When they hurt you and they corner you, maybe blackmail, or murder, is all you've got left."

He sighed. "Try Dilly Salamonica," he replied. "She's living with her sister out in Maryland. The sister takes care of her, I hear. She's occasionally out to lunch, as the story goes." He gave me a number. "They'll know how to reach her."

"Anybody else?"

He thought it over. "Harvey Koppel. Drives a cab in Arlington."

Koppel wouldn't be hard to find. I wrote his name under the first one Charlie had given me. Charlie thought he was finished. I knew him better than that, even after twelve years.

"Who's the one you're holding back, Charlie?"

He tried to look innocent. "Hey, I gave you what I know," he protested.

"Don't kid a kidder, Charlie. You know somebody else. Is somebody still underground?"

Charlie looked suspicious again. "You're sure you aren't working for the cops?"

I finished my drink. "How long have we known each other, Charlie? Twenty years?"

He looked stricken, and I didn't care. Charlie didn't dare stop long enough to think, either about the past or about the future. He'd left his youth in the past, and death lurked in the future.

"Is it the kid, Charlie? Your half-brother? Is he around here now?"

"He's doing okay, Cronyn. Solid guy. Don't make waves for him."

"I won't make waves for anybody."

"He's a customer's man," said Charlie. "I think that's what they call them. He works for a firm uptown. Calls himself Blasingame now." He gave me the name of the firm. It's one of the biggest. "He's a stockbroker," he added, his voice full of disbelief. "A goddamned stockbroker."

I stood up. Charlie was shaking his head in bewilderment, muttering to himself.

"Why not?" I said. "Hayden married a rich movie star and became a politician."

"Hayden was always a politician," said Charlie morosely. "And you became a goddamned private cop."

7

KOPPEL WAS A little guy who wore a cap pulled down over his head and peered out at the world through his steering wheel. He spoke without ever turning around. All I saw of his face were his eyes, occasionally looking back at me through the rear-view mirror.

"Sure, I knew Fromann," he admitted.

"When did you see him last?"

He thought about that. "Four, maybe five months ago, I guess. It was hot," he replied. "I'd dropped a fare out by the courthouse. I saw this guy across the street on Wilson Boulevard, thumbing toward Seven Corners. He looked familiar, so I swung the cab over to him, stuck my head out, and said, 'Hi ya, Ted' and he damn near had a stroke. Hell, Cronyn, I didn't know that he was still down under."

"Then what?"

"I took him out to Seven Corners. He said that he was going to thumb out Route Seven to Leesburg. He'd been living in somebody's horse barn out there. He said the damned horses lived better than he did."

That didn't mesh with the picture I had of Murray Atwood, lounging in sweater and slippers and drinking good Scotch.

"You believed him?"

"Sure. He smelled like a damn horse. Besides, he wanted to know if I could let him have a twenty."

"You give it to him?"

"He needed it worse than I did. He'd been making it

63

on handouts from old friends, so he said. That and whatever he could pick up here and there."

"You haven't seen him since then?"

Koppel hesitated before replying. "No," he said. "Heard from him though. An envelope addressed to me at the cab company came about a month ago. Had a fifty-dollar bill in it and a note thanking me for the twenty and the lift to Seven Corners."

"Did the note indicate how he'd managed to turn things around?"

"No. Nothing else, not even his name, but I knew that it was Ted," Koppel replied. He slowed, looking for the street signs along King Street. "Here's Wakefield," he said and turned into a quiet, curving street.

"This is good enough," I told him. He stopped at the curb, and I handed him a twenty over the back of the seat.

I stepped onto the curb in a quiet neighborhood of renovated brick townhouses with quaint lampposts, their lights twinkling in the clear December air. It looked like a storybook village, an architect's vision of what a colonial village might have looked like if it had all been built by the same developer.

I found the number I wanted and knocked. A man wearing square glasses on a round face that featured a small mouth and protruding eyes opened the door. I stood under the outside light and told him who I was. His tongue wet his lips.

"Yes," he said. "I've been expecting you."

Charlie had called him only twenty minutes earlier, but the man's weary voice sounded as though he had been expecting me for years.

I followed him into a small living room. We stood. I neither heard nor saw anything of the woman whose magazines were so neatly arranged on the mahogany coffee table nor of the child whose cloth dolls occupied each corner of Daddy's big recliner chair.

64

"Ted Fromann is dead," I told the man. "Murdered."
He paled and sagged a little. I went on. "Have you seen
him lately? Say in the last three months?"

"No," he replied. "I haven't seen or heard from Ted in
years, not since . . . ," he paused. He peered at me.
"Charlie says that you're okay, that you were SDS, close
to the top."

"Charlie and I go back a long time."

He thrust both hands into his trouser pockets and
looked at the floor, mentally peeling back the years. He
spoke without looking up.

"Ted was outside man for those kids who blew themselves up," he said. "He knew them better than anybody." A long pause. "We all went underground after
that. I headed for California. I ran into Ted there."

A phone somewhere out of sight rang. He let it ring
three times. Then silence. A signal probably. The unwanted visitor was still there.

"One of those kids had been Ted's girlfriend," the man
went on. "Her death tore him up. He was smoking or
drinking whatever he could get his hands on. Then the
rumor started going around that the FBI had found the
remains of only three of them." He shook his head and
looked up at me. "We tried to tell him, but he wouldn't
listen."

"Tell him what?"

"That the story was an FBI plant, a trap to get us to
raise our heads." He shook his head again. "Ted
wouldn't listen. He loved her too much. He wanted to
believe that she had gotten out. He started spreading the
word where he could be found, hoping that she'd come to
him."

"Instead it was the FBI that arrived," I said.

He nodded. "I had split before then. So had the rest of
us. Ted was nuts; we weren't. I read about them picking
him up. The poor bastard took all the heat. I was glad he
escaped. That's the last I heard of him."

"You're sure about that."

He took off his glasses and rubbed tired eyes. "I was a scared kid, Cronyn, scared and on the run. After Fromann, I was taking no chances on the people I'd been told to rely on. I preferred being on my own. I haven't seen any of them since."

"Where were you yesterday afternoon, say between twelve and three?"

"At my desk. It was a busy day. Check it out. A hundred forty million shares traded on Wall Street."

"Can you prove you were at your desk?"

"Yes, if I have to. All the customer orders I put in have the time recorded. I also keep a time log of all my calls. So do some of my customers. They want to know that their trades are executed promptly."

The phone rang again.

"Answer it," I said. "We're finished. I'll let myself out."

I went out the door to the clear night and the twinkling lights of the storybook village, feeling the seam in time that I had opened for him close behind me.

I used the pay phone to call the Maryland number Charlie had given me. It was a bar. The guy who answered had no trouble telling me where I could find Dilly Salamonica. She lived upstairs over the bar. He said that he'd tell her I was coming, so when I got there forty-five minutes later, she was waiting for me.

Her head barely came up to my shoulders, and she looked like a strong wind would likely blow her over. Her black hair was long and straggly and oily-looking, as though she was waiting for the Redskins to return to the Super Bowl before she washed it.

She looked me over with vague eyes and invited me in from the platform outside her second-story apartment. Inside, the place smelled like she used a lot of onions in her cooking. The jukebox downstairs in the bar played country mostly, it seemed. I couldn't make out the words, but the melody came through the floor and the worn carpet on it.

The door from the platform led into the kitchen of the apartment so we sat there around a formica-topped, chrome-legged table with rings, scratches, and cigarette burns on it. There were only three chairs. Dilly and I occupied two of them.

"Teddy Fromann?" she said, smiling vacantly. "I know Teddy." The smile faded when I told her that he was dead. She turned those vague eyes toward the empty chair by the table. I had the uneasy feeling that she was seeing someone sitting there who I could not see. Fromann maybe.

She spoke without looking at me. In fact it was almost as though she were talking to whoever was in the empty chair.

"Teddy Fromann gone," she said. "Makes me feel all cold." She looked back to me. "Ever have anybody die that you've slept with?" she asked.

"No," I said. "At least, not that I know of."

"It's weird," she said. "Like part of you has gone to wherever the dead person's gone." She eyed me carefully. "What did you come here for?"

"Just to talk," I said.

"That's nice," she said. "Nobody comes to see us. What do you want to talk about?"

"Ted Fromann," I replied.

Her eyes sort of unfocused. She turned to the empty chair. "Ted Fromann's dead," she told it.

"Were you his girlfriend?" I asked her.

She swung the vague eyes back to me. "No," she said. "That was Jenny." She gave the chair another look, as though in confirmation.

I heard the sound of feet mounting the wooden steps outside. The door opened. I sat facing it, always my preference when I have the choice. A woman came through the door and shut it behind her and leaned against it. She wore a blue ski jacket and corduroy pants. She was younger and not so thin as the woman beside me at the table, yet still small. Her hair was also black but worn in a carefully coiffed roll around her neck. I guessed she was the sister.

"Got company, honey?" she asked. The question was directed to the woman at the table but the one at the door looked at me as she asked it.

"Yeah, Mary," she replied. "It's okay. He came to talk with me and Trina about Teddy Fromann."

"I see," said Mary, still eyeing me. "You ought not talk too much about the old days, you know that it makes you tired."

"Oh," she said. She looked at me. "I don't want to get tired." She giggled. "God knows why."

"About Ted Fromann," I repeated, feeling a sense of futility creep over me. It was a strange conversation we were having. Most of the time she looked at the empty chair while Mary and I looked at each other. "Have you seen him lately?"

"Sure," she said. "Let me think." She thought it over without success. "When was it?" she asked the empty chair. Her tone was a little cross. "Maybe last week," she said. "Was that it?"

"You're not so great on time, Dilly," said Mary. She leaned against the door, her hands in her jacket pockets, looking at me.

"Doesn't make any difference," Dilly said and smiled sweetly. "He's dead. I feel weird, Mary. Real weird."

"That's okay, honey. It'll pass. You know it always does. This Fromann fella. He's somebody you used to know?"

"Oh, yes," she said. "Trina knows him too, but she won't tell." A tear came to each eye. "Trina went away for a long time," she said to me. "I miss her. She was so warm in bed beside me. When she was gone, I felt so cold." She looked at the chair. "I miss you," she said, quietly.

I looked at Mary, standing by the door. She bit at her lower lip, and she watched her sister, patiently, with restraint.

I spoke to Dilly once more. "What did you and Fromann talk about?" I asked her.

The vague eyes swung in a lazy arc back to me. "Everything," she said. "The war, I guess. It's everywhere. Even back home. We're all going to die, like those kids last week at the college back home."

She had me there. I looked at the sister. "Where's home?" I asked her.

"Ohio," said Mary.

I turned back to Dilly. "You mean Kent State?" Dilly nodded. "That's been a long time ago," I said.

"Oh." She smiled that sweet smile once more. "What did you say your name was?"

"Cronyn," I replied.

"Cronyn," she repeated. "That's a nice name. Do you know that people can come back from the dead, Cronyn?"

"I didn't know that, Dilly," I said. I kept my eyes away from the empty chair.

A pout replaced the smile. "It's true," she insisted. "I don't care if you get mad at me. It's true."

"Dilly . . ." began the sister.

"No. No." Voice rising now. Anger. Compressed lips. A small fist clenched. "I won't tell you anymore, Mary. Go away. Both of you go away. I don't want to talk to you anymore."

"You talked to Ted Fromann," I reminded her.

"That's different. Teddy said it was all right. That dead people can come back, sometimes." Dilly looked at the empty chair. "But Trina can't come back, because there isn't anything left of her to come back. Oh, Trina, Trina. I loved you so much." She started to cry.

The sister moved further into the room. "Heard enough, Mister?"

I looked up at her. "Yeah," I said, hearing my own voice sound tired. I stood up.

"Wait for me downstairs," she said.

I nodded and went out the door and down the wooden stairs to the cracked sidewalk that ran along the side of the building. I went into the barroom and stood at the bar with a draft beer until the sister joined me. I got us each one and followed her to a booth of plain dark wood.

A man and a woman in their twenties stood at the jukebox trying to make a selection. Three men stood at the bar. Apart from them and the bartender, we had the place to ourselves.

"She's not always like that," Mary said. "It comes and goes. She can be really okay sometimes."

"You're her sister?" I asked. She nodded. "She needs help," I told her.

"I can look after her," Mary replied. "They talked about putting her someplace but I'll be damned if they're going to lock her up." She paused. "Just leave my sister to me, will you, and let's talk about you and this person Fromann."

"Did you know him?"

"No," she replied. Understanding crossed her face. "He's past tense?"

"Yes," I replied. "Murdered yesterday."

She stared at me for a long moment during which the jukebox came to life. "Did you tell Dilly?"

"Only that he's dead. Not how."

"Thanks," she said. "Are you a cop?"

"No. Private investigator."

She thought that over and nodded. She looked at me, nice eyes, green, full of concern. "Who was he?"

"Radical, fugitive, blackmailer. In that order, over time. Years ago he was tight with four young people who formed the most dangerous bomb group the FBI had to contend with. One of those people was named Trina, Katrina Onders."

"Yes," Mary said, her voice hardly audible above the sound of Tammy Wynette coming from the jukebox.

My own memory was not faultless. I remembered some of the names, not all. Katrina Onders and Mike something, last name forgotten. Jenny something, last name also forgotten. Robbie Dempsey was the one I remembered best. He'd been the youngest. I could remember the poem that had appeared in the alternative press. "Ode to Robbie" or "Glory in the Death of a Young Revolutionary," something like that. It had been a long time ago.

"Don't bother her," said Mary.

"I need to ask her some questions," I said. "When does she have a good spell?"

Mary shook her head. "Keep her out of it. Whatever trouble you're carrying let my sister alone. She can't help you."

"You can't keep her out of it. She was connected to Fromann in the past, and she may have seen him recently."

She pushed her glass of beer away from her. "No," she said. "No, dammit. Just leave her alone." She started to slide out of the booth.

I grabbed her wrist and held her. "A man is dead, Mary, a man who was your sister's friend. Don't you care about that? Don't you think that she would care?"

She stopped pulling away from me. The bartender had appeared by the side of the booth. He was a fat guy wearing a long, white apron tied around his gut. His right hand was under the apron. He probably held a blackjack or a length of pipe. He looked at me as he spoke to her.

"Everything cool here, Mary?"

71

She looked up at him as I allowed her to disengage. "Yeah, Rick, everything's cool."

He looked relieved and glad to head for the bar again.

We sat in silence for a while before she asked, "What do you want?"

"I'm looking for some letters written to Fromann by a woman. If he has spoken to your sister recently, he may have mentioned them. He may also have mentioned if anyone else knew about those letters. They're missing. Your sister may be able to help me find them."

"No," she said. "I don't care about you or any letters. All I care about is her."

I leaned back against the hard back of the booth, pulling my beer toward me. "All right," I said. I had pushed her to the wall. I couldn't push farther. "I won't hurt your sister."

She put her elbows on the table between us and put her face into her hands.

"What was it, Mary?" I asked the top of her head. "LSD?"

She straightened up and took a deep breath and nodded. A long sigh accompanied the nod. Some of the tenseness seemed to flow out of her body. "That's part of it," she replied. "I've heard that it short-circuits some of the connections in the brain. With Dilly, the short-circuits seem permanent."

"Dilly never had it all together, did she?"

The sister looked down into her glass. "No, not really," she replied. "Mom and Dad didn't want to believe that, and who can blame them? Everybody liked Dilly. Mom said that she was born with a sweet disposition. One of the sisters at school told Mom that Dilly had an inner glow. If you were a mother what would you believe? That your kid had a screw loose or that she had an inner glow?"

It was a question that needed no answer. I gave her a

moment to swallow some beer before asking her my own question.

"You said that the LSD was part of it. What was the other part?"

"I think that it's that girl she talks about. Trina. My sister was talking to her at the very moment when that house where Trina lived blew up. She's never gotten over it." Mary paused for more beer. She took a deep breath and exhaled. "I really don't understand two women," she went on, "being, well, together like that." She looked at me, her eyes questioning what for her would be forever unknowable. "You know what I mean?"

I nodded. I didn't need to say anything.

"But Dilly's my sister, and she loved that girl." She looked away. "They say that Onders was blown into little red chunks of meat. My sister lives with that memory." She finished the last of the beer in her glass.

I went to the bar and returned with another for each of us. The bartender pretended he'd never seen me before.

"I was in high school," Mary continued, "when she went away. I was trying to be the perfect daughter and not doing too well."

"An older sister with an inner glow is a tough act to follow."

Mary did, after all, know how to smile. She showed me that she did. It was a nice smile, a little like her sister's smile but more thoughtful, more knowing.

A memory came along and drove the smile away. "Mom and Dad and other people," she said, "were beginning to notice things, but they pretended the screwy things she did weren't her fault, or that they never happened. And we never talked to each other about her. That was probably the worst; everybody being afraid to admit that they'd seen something in Dilly that couldn't be explained by the inner glow."

"Such as?"

Mary shrugged. "Ever wonder where she came up with the name of Dilly?" She didn't wait for an answer. "She was baptized Theresa. Before she left Ohio, she started carrying a flower with her everywhere she went, and she wanted people to call her Daffodil. Hence, Dilly. Eventually she went away, to help bring peace and love to the world."

"Not a bad thing to try to do."

"Big deal," she said. "What did it get her? What did it get anybody?"

"I don't know." It was the same answer I always gave myself. Maybe if we'd all been as innocent as Dilly, I'd have had a different answer. "You think she could have been helped before she went away?"

"Maybe. Anyway it was too late after the wine and the pot and the acid and the freedom to do your own thing," she said. "And after Katrina Onders."

"Your parents never knew?"

"They'd die, Cronyn."

The parents were still back in Ohio, apparently still telling themselves that everything was fine with their eldest daughter.

"And what about you?" I asked her.

She smiled again, a small, sad smile. She had come to Washington in response to a plea from Dilly for help. She hadn't done anything to amount to before leaving Ohio and precious little since, at least so she said.

There had been a husband in her past, one she didn't want to talk about, I guessed. She mentioned it in passing only, just to explain that she went by her married name of Thresher. The husband, I gathered, was ancient history. Coming to Washington seemed at the time to be a good opportunity to put her own life back together, only no one then had known how bad Dilly was getting.

"I was shocked," Mary told me. "She's worse now, but even then I was not prepared for the way she was."

Mary stayed to help her sister regain her old self, shielding the extent of Dilly's problem from the rest of the family, hoping that Dilly would recover. Months lengthened into years with Dilly slipping backward. Mary's hope for her sister's recovery crumbled, to be replaced by a prayer that Dilly would become no worse, a prayer that, unanswered, dissolved into resignation and led to a life of unremitting sacrifice for the younger sister.

Mary didn't tell me that in so many words. You had to go behind the words. She maintained the ever-present denial of herself. Dilly's needs were paramount, at the expense of Mary, to the extent necessary, and it grew gradually more and more necessary. She told me about herself calmly, without self-pity, without any understanding of how Dilly's illness was consuming not one but two lives.

She emptied her glass. "I have to get back upstairs," she said. "Thanks for the beer. Two are my limit."

"And about Dilly and Fromann?" I asked.

She fixed me with a direct look, firm and steady. "Leave us alone, Cronyn."

"I'm not sure I can do that, Mary."

She stood up. "I don't want to fight you, Cronyn, but I'll do what I have to."

"It's not just me," I told her. "This thing may not let you duck it."

"I can try," she said.

"It may be too late. Dilly may be into it too deeply. Suppose Fromann did come here recently? Maybe not last week, as she said, but sometime since he surfaced in D. C.? The cops may get onto that. What then?"

Her face reflected despair. "I don't know," she said and left.

8

ON WEDNESDAY MORNING I made it a point to look for
Ralph, the major-domo of the lobby, part guard and part
janitor. He had been ducking me, I think, but on this
occasion I found him sitting in his little room off the
lobby, watching the flickering screen of a four-inch television set. I stood in the doorway. He was trying to
pretend that I wasn't there.

I said, "The next time you let a cop into my office
without me being there, he'd better show you a warrant
first. Don't get me mad at you, Ralphie."

I was about halfway to the elevator when he caught up
to me, apologizing, sorry as all hell and promising never
to do it again. He'd had just enough time to remember
that Christmas was coming and that event usually meant
a hundred from me.

He tried to make amends in the only way he knew
how, by telling me that I had a visitor waiting for me in
the snack bar. "Young white dude," he said. "Big
mother. Smells like a girl."

"Tell him to come up," I said, after which I walked to
the elevator and rode it up to the floor where I do
business. My office consists of one room only, and the
door to that room from the corridor is locked when I'm
not there. The door has a mail slot in it, and a pad and
pencil next to it for the convenience of clients who drop
by when I'm not there.

That seldom happens, which is one reason I dispense
with a secretary. Another reason is the ten or twelve
thousand a year I'd have to pay her. Potential clients

usually, but not always, get my number from the phone book, and then they pick up A.G. Bell's brainstorm and make an appointment, the same as they would if they had a toothache and needed a dentist.

I unlocked the door to the office and went to the men's room, figuring that my visitor couldn't be too dangerous if he smelled like a girl. When I returned I saw that he had taken advantage of the open door. He sat, relaxed, in one of the chairs in front of the desk. A scarf and gloves lay on the corner of the desk. I saw no coat or hat. The sound of my closing the door drew his attention.

He turned in the chair and smiled. He casually stood up, all six-five of him. I didn't see any slack under the bulging shoulders or narrow waist of his custom tweed sports jacket, and I didn't see any fat either. I had to guess that he probably weighed in at 275.

He wore jeans that stretched tightly around muscular thighs. I doubted that he could have worn dress slacks without stretching the crease right out of them. He also wore a year-round tan. Above it flowed thick, golden hair, fashionably styled and cut. He was, I guessed, twenty-three or twenty-four.

I saw all those things quickly, and they registered. Yet those were only details. It was his face that caught your attention. An artist might reach for his brushes and paints; a poet for pencil and paper. All I can say is that if you could stuff that body into a dress, you'd have about the most beautiful woman you ever saw.

"Hi," he said, taking a step toward me and extending his big right hand to be shaken. "I'm Taffy."

That was all. Just "Taffy." I took his hand, gave it a pump, and let go. At close range, he smelled nice. Too nice, I thought. I went to my chair behind the desk, and we both sat down.

"You're Cronyn?" he said, making sure. He was still smiling.

78

"That's right. What can I do for you?"

"A woman came to you Monday," he said. "Her name is Paula Devlin. I want to know why she should need to engage the services of a private investigator."

Taffy talked like someone trying to imitate the characters in a television play imported from the BBC. I had a hunch that among friends in more relaxed moments, Taffy had a gutsier line of patter. Which, consequently, led me to think that Taffy wasn't as relaxed as he looked.

"Sorry, I can't help you," I said in my politest tone.

He went on as though I hadn't said anything. "She would have most certainly used an alias," he told me. "You would not have forgotten her, however. You might even have thought that she was attractive." For a moment the amiable veneer slipped, and a spiteful side of beautiful Taffy peeked out.

"She dresses expensively," he went on, describing Paula Devlin in his own way, "but colorlessly, mostly grays and blacks. She has black hair worn to collar length. She is taller than the average woman with a well-proportioned body, at least for her age." Meow-meow. "She says that she is thirty-six years old."

"Don't know the lady," I said. "Sorry."

The smile on his pretty face almost surrendered to a pout. "She was here," he pointed out.

"Then ask her."

"I'm asking you."

"Fair enough. You've asked, and I told you."

"You're lying. You're protecting her."

"Look, Taffy," I said pleasantly. "I've been accused of a lot worse than that. In my business you learn to take it. It's just part of what I have to put up with in order to keep the bank account healthy. But I don't have to be agreeable when it's for free, so if you aren't a little nicer, I'm going to have to ask you to leave."

If the threat implicit in my words bothered him, he

didn't show it. He probably thought he could take me. He had the size to do it, but you never know for sure until you try.

A knowing look crossed his pretty face. "I do require your assistance," he said, choosing his words, "but I do not expect you to provide it without reimbursement."

"I guess that means you'll pay me, is that it?"

"Exactly."

"How much?" I asked and tried to look greedy.

Taffy's face showed his attempt to calculate silently the right amount needed to buy me. He took a folded wallet from his outside jacket pocket, opened it, and looked inside. He extracted a couple of bills and extended his arm to lay them on my desk. He hands were the size of hams.

I picked up the two bills. They were twenties. Taffy's face carried a satisfied expression that told me what he thought I was worth. "Tell you what, Taffy," I said as I rolled the bills into a ball and tossed the ball to him. He caught it neatly in one quick snatch that showed me fast reflexes. "You take that and shove it and get the hell out of here before I call the one-legged janitor and have him throw you out."

Taffy looked at me and then at the balled-up wad in his hand. He carefully unfolded each bill and put them back into his wallet. He looked up at me and smiled, holding up both hands in a peace gesture. "No hard feelings, I hope. I was just asking, you know." He smiled even more prettily.

"I know what that's like," I said pleasantly. He seemed to have gotten the message that I either didn't know Paula Devlin, or if I did I wasn't about to talk about her.

Taffy stood up. "I appreciate it, Mr. Cronyn. I really do appreciate it. You've been decent about my coming here." He extended his hand, tentatively, as though he feared a rebuff.

I stood up too, but I ignored the proffered hand. "It's okay."

He looked down at his hand. "I guess you don't want to shake on it. I mean, on no hard feelings."

"Just take my word for it."

"I'm sorry you feel that way," he said. "It hurts, you know. It hurts a lot to be treated like you have some kind of disease because you're gay."

"Look, Taffy . . ." I began.

"I'm human too, you know. I have feelings the same as anybody. Don't you care, Mr. Cronyn?"

There wasn't anything to say to that. It's your actions that show whether you are ruled by prejudices or you're not. Words don't count. I stuck out my hand.

He smiled into my eyes and for the next second and a half I wasn't sure what was going on.

Whatever happened, happened fast, and I found myself lying across my desk. He had both of my arms bent behind me and seemed determined to see if the shoulder sockets would give enough for me to scratch my neck with my thumbs.

I tried using my head to butt him in the crotch but he was having none of that. He threatened to twist off the arms and hand them to me, one at a time. I didn't know whether he could do that or not, but I was in no position to risk it. I ceased and desisted from further efforts to get out of his grip.

"You're a mean, evil shit," said Taffy, no longer trying to talk like BBC.

"I'm okay when you get to know me," I replied between clenched teeth.

He moved my arms higher. I groaned despite an unspoken resolve not to.

"The woman, what's she paying you for?"

"Don't . . . know . . . the . . . lady," I replied. I would have liked to have added, "Sorry, old man." It might have reminded Taffy of his politer mood. But I didn't, couldn't really. It's just hard to talk when you'd rather yell.

Taffy didn't say anything for a moment that seemed like an eternity to me. If my mind had not been entirely preoccupied with the agony in my arms and shoulders, I might have tried to anticipate his next move. As it was, when he let my arms drop free, it took me by surprise.

No matter. My arms were useless anyway. They hung numbly to my sides in the brief instant while he went around the desk and got me from behind. His arms went under my shoulders, and he clasped his hands behind my head. He pulled my shoulders toward him, arching my back, and he pressed my head down against the wall. I felt like a pretzel.

"I followed her here, Cronyn," he said, "and I want to know why she came or I'll break you in two."

He could do it. I held no illusions about that. Whether he would or not was another matter. My brain returned to its post after he had released my arms. The position in which he held me was awkward, dangerous, and painful, but not as painful as the prior one. I could think, and I could talk, not easily with my chin on my chest, but I could say what I had to.

"Life is what you get for murder, Taffy," I said. "The guard downstairs. He'll remember you."

"It won't do you any good, shit."

"Right. But what good's a threat to kill me, Taffy, if I don't think you're ready to do the kind of hard time you'll get for it?"

That gave him something to think about, but it wasn't enough. He had to doubt his certainty. And he also had to have a reasonable story, one which would work for him. Otherwise he might not kill me, he'd just think of some other fun game to play, eye-gouging or castration maybe.

"She must have visited another office," I said.

"The elevator light stopped at this floor," he retorted and pushed my head forward for emphasis.

"There are four other offices on this floor, including a tax accountant and an employment agency. She could have gone to any one of them. Hell's fire, man, you don't think I'd be crazy enough to risk a broken neck just over a damned woman, do you? I don't hire out my life, only my time."

That made sense to Taffy. Who would believe that a forty-dollar-an-hour private dick with a dingy office in a worn-out building would risk his life for a client? Not even I believed it, and I didn't want to think about what I'd have done if I couldn't have talked Taffy out of breaking my neck.

He wasn't quite finished with me. He pushed me forward to the wall and banged my head against the hard plaster twice, just for the fun of it. Pinwheels of dazzling lights shot through my skull. He then steered me, staggering, to my chair, released me, and pushed me down into it.

With arms hanging down and through unfocused eyes, I watched him twirl his scarf around his neck. He tossed a business card on my desk. "If she comes here, I want to know about it," he told me, slipping on his gloves. "You can leave a message for me at that number." He grinned at me. "You ought to retire, Cronyn. You're getting too old for this stuff." He giggled and went out the door.

I didn't say anything. I just sat there, and the blood crept down my cheeks from the cuts on my scalp, while I let the fog in my brain evaporate.

When I thought I could, I stood up. The stomach was a little queasy, and when I managed to reach the men's room, breakfast came up. I washed my face and cleaned the wounds and staunched the blood and looked into the mirror to a face whiter than usual.

Paula Devlin's friends played rough. Just ask me. Or Ted Fromann.

She called while my head was still hurting and said that she wanted to see me. She didn't want to come to the office, so I told her where we could meet and when.

I tried Walter Devlin's office again and got precisely nowhere with his secretary. She told me his calendar was full and that I should tell her what I wanted. I declined to do that, her voice became more haughty, and I hung up, unwilling to argue with her. Devlin would see me, whether his secretary okayed it or not. In the meantime, I decided that I needed a little background on brother Devlin.

I started with my source book, so called because it contains the names and numbers of people who know a lot more about their little niches in Washington than one person could possibly know. The first two calls netted me nothing. On the third, I found someone who had heard of the name Devlin. On the fourth, I found the source I needed.

"Walter Devlin, Sammy," I said into the telephone. "Know him?"

"Sure, watcha think?"

Sammy runs a one-man news service out of Washington, D.C., specializing in safety issues. There's a lot of that sort of thing being done, and it's guys like Sammy who often break the first word of hanky-panky in the government. Some of Sammy's most faithful subscribers are the hot-shot investigative reporters for the *Post* and the *Times* and *The Wall Street Journal,* not to mention the famous faces you see on the networks.

"What are you chewing on?" I asked, curious.

"Lunch," said Sammy.

"It's ten o'clock," I pointed out.

"So it's breakfast."

Sammy sits still only long enough to write his newsletter. The rest of the time he's on the go. I think he probably works in his sleep.

"So what's with you and Devlin?" Sammy wanted to know. "You got something for me?"

"I might eventually," I said. "What about Devlin? I called two other sources before you, and they had never heard of him."

"He keeps a low profile."

"If he keeps a low profile, how does he get clients?"

"It's not that low," replied Sammy, chewing. "He has an office on Connecticut Avenue."

"I can find that out from the telephone book," I said. "The next thing is for you to tell me that he wants people to think he's a management consultant. Is that the sort of thing people pay you an outrageous subscription price for?"

"You aren't paying," he pointed out. Pause. Then, "On the other hand . . ."

Sammy had once turned up some damning evidence against a greedy congressman. Unfortunately for Sammy, the congressman had some mean and evil friends. They had it in mind to break Sammy's legs, though he hadn't known that when he asked me to go with him to a meeting with the congressman at a farm on the Eastern Shore. The congressman's two friends joined us. Things became a little complicated and when it was over, the only one left at the farm was the congressman, dead of a heart attack. Sammy never wanted to talk about that night, and he was grateful that I never did.

"Devlin's a pointer and door-opener, Danny. Say you're a businessman from Chitlinswitch and you have a problem with the government. You come here to try to straighten it out. Now, you may be a big cheese in Chitlinswitch, and you may know all there is to know about your business, but you come here and man, you ain't shit. You need to talk to the right people but hell, you can't even *find* the right people, and even if you could, they don't know you. That's where a guy like Devlin comes in. You tell him your problem, play eighteen holes of golf at Devlin's club, and get up the next morning ready to present your side of the problem to the people who can do something about it, which is all you ever wanted to do in the first place."

"If it were that easy, I'd be doing what Devlin does," I said, "instead of trying to get information from somebody who doesn't know whether he's eating lunch or breakfast."

"You got too many rough edges for that type of work, Danny boy."

"You're saying that Devlin's a smoothie."

"As Vaseline," he replied and thought it over. "Teflon, maybe," he amended. "Nothing sticks to him."

"Is there anything to stick?"

I listened to a long silence on the telephone.

"All I know is what I hear," said Sammy, at last.

"Good enough."

"Devlin came to D.C. about ten, maybe twelve, years ago," Sammy began. "Nobody I've talked to knows for sure what for, but the best guess is that some Miami interests sent him up here to look after things."

"What things?"

"Small-time rackets. Bootleg booze, numbers, prostitution, pornography, that sort of thing. The Miami interests hoped to organize the small-time stuff. According to people who'll talk about it, it didn't work out. As best as I can tell, Devlin dropped out of sight for a year or so, before surfacing as a consultant."

"Clean?"

"As a hound's tooth. Apparently he had severed all his connections with the Miami boys, though he did start his consulting business with a couple of banana republics as clients. His Miami connections could have helped him with that."

"He'd have had to register under the Foreign Agents Law."

"Yeah," said Sammy, his voice dry. "He overlooked that, and the Feds got on his back. He dropped his foreign clients. By then he had a start with his U.S. customers. His list just kept right on growing."

"What makes him so good?"

"Personal attention to his contacts in the government. He's built up a pretty loyal following, so I hear. He'll never let a friend be lonely at a party, for example. Walter would know of a girl, or boy, to help chase the blues away. Walter's no pimp, of course, he just knows where the answer to your problems can be found. Want a toot? Betcha he'd have a phone number for that, too. You have to make your own deal or your own date, but if you were interested in that sort of action, wouldn't you like to have a friend like Walter? Any of this helping you?"

"I don't know," I told him, truthfully. "Ever hear the name Murray Atwood used in connection with Devlin?"

"No, not that I recall. Who is Atwood?"

"A corpse." I told him about the murder. Sammy once told me that he read eight newspapers and two magazines every day. When you cover that much ground, you have to be fast to pick out only those things you need to know. Sammy didn't have time for the crime news.

"Walter Devlin as the enraged jealous husband?" asked Sammy. "I'll believe that on the day the Senators come back to RFK Stadium. Hell, Danny, Devlin's got a nice little business going. He's not the type to fuck that up over a woman. He can always get another wife."

"What do his contacts do for him in return?" I asked.

"Listen to his clients. I hear that Devlin is selective about his clients. The client has to have a problem in an area where Devlin's government contacts can help."

I thought that one over for a few seconds. "You mean that he has a few select people on his payroll?"

"No, nothing like that. Devlin's too smart for that. He's in this for the long haul. Bribery is a shortcut to Atlanta. Besides, I know some of his contacts. They may like their personal brand of sin but they're smart enough not to break the law helping Devlin's clients."

"But they do help his clients."

"Sure. They like Walter. They also know that Walter is not going to send them somebody who out and out wants them to break regulations or law. Walter deals only with people who have a legitimate case to present, people who seek a remedy that comes from administrative interpretation. Hell, that happens a thousand times a day. What the hell do you think bureaucrats do?"

"I know what they do. We've created such a mess that we have to employ several hundreds of thousands of mostly honest men and women paid by the taxpayer to try to figure it out. Then we have more hundreds of thousands of mostly honest men and women also paid by the taxpayer to fight with the first bunch over the same turf. And on top of that we employ another hundred thousand to second-guess all the others."

"It keeps the taxpayers' money in circulation, Danny."

"And keeps guys like Devlin in business," I said. I asked about Sammy's wife and three teenage daughters, promised to have lunch with him in the indefinite future and hung up.

I stood up and stretched, walked around the room and stared out the window, walked around the desk twice and wound up in front of one of the chalk drawings. Their creator had been in town after Thanksgiving, according to a brief piece in the *Post*. She hadn't called. I knew where she could have been reached but I hadn't called either. When it's over, it's over.

I went back to the desk and sat down. Devlin. Think about Devlin. What's to think about? He wasn't breaking any laws that I knew about, and he didn't sound like the type to go off on a shooting spree because his wife had hopped into bed with someone else. People like him have too much to lose.

You read about the ones who do pop their corks and chill the wife or husband, but they aren't the Devlins of this world. They are usually obscure little people with the sanity ground out of them by a vast anonymous society that they don't understand, by a system that seems to give them no control over their own destiny, and by a bizarre and whimsical Fate that seems to block them at every turn. Something snaps in them when the frustrations become unbearable and the rage intolerable, and they take a rifle or shotgun or pistol and destroy the faithless spouse who for the moment represents the totality of Life's Dirty Tricks.

But these are people who feel they haven't any more to lose, that life has betrayed them for the last time. Not Devlin. He'd have too much to lose. Like Sammy said, Devlin could always get another wife.

So if jealousy seemed to be an unlikely reason to motivate Devlin to murder, what else? The letters. His wife's good name. I gave that one a maybe and not too strong a one. It looked better if you extended it to Devlin himself, that is, a scandal that would make him look like a fool. That could hurt business, and Devlin had, according to Sammy, come out of a background that took very seriously anything that would hurt business.

That sounded better but I had to ask myself if a man who allegedly strained at the gnat of bribery would so easily swallow the camel of murder. I answered myself that he might, but only if Atwood could do far worse than make Devlin look foolish. If those "Miami interests" trusted Devlin as a possible organizer, you could bet that he had learned how to handle a genuine threat to business.

All of that occupied my mind for a while but it didn't tell me who had Paula Devlin's hot, throbbing letters. I had two names: Walter Devlin, cuckolded husband, and Carlos Ramirez, rejected ex-lover. It wasn't much of a start. Ramirez said he'd never heard of the dead man and showed genuine ignorance of the letters. Having come up with nothing from the ex-lover, I hoped to do better with the husband. If I could get in to see him.

In the meantime I took two aspirin and went to see what Paula Devlin wanted.

9

SHE CAME OUT of the Smithsonian subway station into the dull, gray cold of the day and stood there surveying the vastness of the Mall around her, taking her bearings. She wore a gray down-filled, nylon jacket, black cap, black skirt, and leather boots. She started walking along Jefferson Drive, following instructions.

I started the engine of the station wagon and crept forward slowly until the car and I were abreast of her. Behind us the Washington Monument rose in slender grandeur, its top blurred by a low-hanging haze.

"Mrs. Devlin."

She jerked around to face me. Her breathing left little clouds of vapor around her face.

She came around the station wagon and got in on the passenger side. I moved us forward a few hundred feet to a bus zone and shut off the engine and looked at her.

She went right to the point. "A messenger service delivered the letters today." She paused. Something about her voice told me not to be too happy too soon. She went on, "I burned them."

"Thanks," I said. "You knew damned well those letters would get me off the hook with the cops."

She said she was sorry, but it didn't sound like she was. "They would have ruined me," she explained. "I have comfort and security and a husband who makes few demands. I intend to keep what I have. Going with you to the police and confessing an unfortunate love affair would ruin everything. The letters are gone. If the police think you are lying to them about Murray having a mistress who wrote indiscreet letters, I shall be happy to confirm for them that you are a liar. I shall have never met you, Mr. Cronyn."

"It seems as though you are in the driver's seat," I conceded. "If you need me as a witness against your late lover for having attempted blackmail, all you need to do is call me. I would have to back up that story since it's the one I gave to the police. On the other hand, I can't take the initiative to link you to the dead man because the letters are gone."

She thought that over, looking out through the windshield. Ahead of us, a large, orange bus stopped, red lights flashing at its corners. Its doors opened, disgorging a stream of six-year-olds onto the Mall. Two young women lined them up by twos, each pair holding hands, and they marched off to see the dinosaurs in the Museum of Natural History.

She turned toward me. "Understand this, Mr. Cronyn. Walter's business demands a great deal of contact with people. I play a role in that, and I do it well enough that Walter has never had any cause for complaint."

"You help him entertain the visiting businessmen. Keep the clients happy, that sort of thing."

"Yes, when the situation calls for a hostess. Mostly though, my duties are with the wives. Walter's clients come to town to transact business with the government. Walter helps them, and he keeps them very busy."

"And while the busy businessman goes here and there, passing through the doors that Devlin opens, the businessman's good wife cannot be left alone in a hotel room. Is that it?"

"I try to be a companion, a friend," she replied. "These women are on their own in a strange city. If I suggest a shopping trip downtown, or lunch, or a matinee at the Kennedy Center, they usually jump at it." She paused. "You see my problem."

"Yeah," I said. My voice was dry. "You wouldn't look so genteel to the visiting wives. No help to good old Walt in his business. He'd dump you." I looked at her carefully. "What about Ramirez? I told him about the letters."

She gave me a faint smile. "He doesn't believe I'd do such a thing."

"You've talked to him?"

"He called. He said that you had gone to see him. Naturally he believed me rather than you."

"Naturally," I said. She started out of the car as though our conversation was finished. It wasn't. "By the way, Mrs. Devlin, I bumped into Taffy this morning."

She stopped and turned to face me. She stared for a moment, her eyes reflecting her struggle to find something to say. Finally, she said, tentatively, "I didn't realize you knew him."

"Only slightly," I replied. "It's a small world, wouldn't you say?"

She tried to smile. It didn't work. "Did he mention me?" she asked.

"Yes. Your name did come up in the conversation. He seemed certain that you and I were acquainted."

"I see," she said. "What did you tell him about me?"

"Not much. He seems to know you a great deal better than I do." I paused innocently. "I don't think he likes you, Mrs. Devlin. Did you know that?"

"He hates me," she replied in a tight voice. "He works for my husband," she added. "More than that, really. He is my rival."

I knew that my eyebrows must have shown a noticeable rise. "For your husband's affections?"

"I don't know. Possibly Taffy may think so. I meant

rivals in a business sense. I help Walter with his consultant business. Taffy . . . ," she hesitated. "I'm not sure what Taffy does. It's almost as though there is another side to Walter's affairs. Taffy helps on that side."

She didn't say what side that was. I had the feeling she knew more about it than she was telling.

"And now Taffy doesn't think that that's enough," I suggested. "He wants to be number one boy, period."

She nodded.

"To achieve that, he has to get you out of the way."

She nodded again. "That's right."

I considered her carefully. "You're an intelligent woman, with the added benefit of having mature, experienced judgment. I wouldn't give Taffy a chance, myself, not on your respective merits."

"It will not be decided on merit," she said, "but on loyalty. Walter is a fanatic on loyalty. And he can't conceive of a wife who sleeps with another man as being loyal. To him, such a woman's first loyalty is always to her lover."

Something that Ramirez had said clicked over in my mind, something about her having been afraid an enemy had discovered their affair. He hadn't said who. Now I thought I knew. I told her what Ramirez had said and asked, "Taffy?"

She nodded again. "Yes. He tried to trap me. It was a clumsy effort. I made him look like a fool. Walter was quite upset with him for his juvenile jealousies. Taffy nearly lost his own place with Walter."

"I'd say that he's determined to nail you this time."

She looked worried. "What did you tell him?"

"Nothing. I don't like it when some barrelhead gets the notion that he can buy me," I replied. Especially, I thought, for forty dollars. "It's bad business."

The look she gave me seemed to say that she was trying to make up her mind whether to believe that.

"You're in the clear," I told her. "With the letters gone, well, I'll have a hell of a time explaining to the cops, but I don't see what more I can do about it."

She still didn't look as though she believed me, and I didn't much care. I turned away and started the car and said, "Good-bye, Mrs. Devlin."

I went back to my office and ate lunch at my desk, having picked up a ham sandwich, a cup of bean soup, and a pint of chocolate milk from the snack bar on the ground floor as I came into the building. I'd spent the better part of a month on the street or in other people's homes and offices, working twelve- and fourteen-hour days for paying clients, before the corpse of Ted Fromann came into my life. As a result of all that activity, my desk needed attention. Letters waited to be answered, bills to be paid, filing to be done, a bank statement to be reconciled, and, worst of all, reports to be written.

Paula Devlin's burning the letters had left me with nothing else to do but to face the mess in my office. I squared off and tackled the job with as much gusto as I could muster, putting Paula Devlin and the rest of them out of my mind for the moment. Accomplishment rewarded effort, and by mid-afternoon I had everything neatly organized, filed, and otherwise taken care of.

My bank statement informed me that the labors of the previous weeks had not been in vain. I leaned back in my chair, clasped my hands together behind my neck and contemplated how I might spend the fruits of those labors and, in so doing, increase the holiday joy of the local merchants.

A knock at the door interrupted my reverie. I went to the door and opened it, and I read the look on Mary Thresher's face as she stood there, a look that told me I had not yet done with Ted Fromann.

*   *   *

She sat in one of the chairs across the desk from me. "It's Dilly," she said. "She insists on going to the police." She hesitated. "She says that she is responsible for Fromann's death. Something about tampering with things beyond the grave."

"It's hard to get a cop to pay attention to the hereafter," I suggested.

"It's not just that," she replied. She hesitated. I waited. She went on. "Fromann did come to see her, about three months ago. She was clear about it. And I also remembered something. It was my birthday. Dilly always buys me something, a record usually. That time, though, she said she was out of money, that she had loaned her last seventeen dollars to an old friend."

Mary took an envelope from her purse. It had Dilly's name and address on the outside and had been postmarked about a month before. "Look inside," said Mary, handing it to me.

I did. The envelope contained four fifty-dollar bills clipped to a scrap of yellow, lined paper. On the paper were the words "Thanks for the help" and the initials "TF." I handed it all back to Mary. "From Fromann."

"Yes. Dilly gave it to me, as proof that she really had talked to him."

"It fits. She wasn't the only one he'd borrowed from lately, and whom he had repaid generously. In Dilly's case, though, it's almost as though she did something else for him. Has she said what?"

Again the shake of the head. "The only thing she says is that they talked about old friends. She became angry when I pressed her. She said that I wouldn't believe her anyway. I asked her if she'd talk to you about it, and she said that you were no better than I. I don't know what she meant by that."

"But she'd tell the police?"

Mary hesitated before answering. "What could she tell them?"

"I don't know. Do you want me to go with her to the police? Maybe that would help."

"No," she answered. "She can't go to them."

I considered her carefully. "What aren't you telling me, Mary? What are you holding back?"

"Nothing," she replied, too quickly.

"What were her exact words?" I asked. Mary stared at the edge of my desk, not answering. "Did she say that she was responsible for Ted Fromann's death?" I paused. "Or did she say that she had killed Ted Fromann?"

A long silence. Then, "Yes. That she killed him."

I stood up and went to the water cooler and fetched a cup of water for each of us. I sat on the corner of my desk and handed her one of the cups. "Do you want a drink?" I offered.

She declined. She looked into my eyes. "Will you take what I've told you to the police?"

"No, not if you don't want me to."

She let out a long breath. "I told you that I'd take care of it," she said.

"I remember."

"I can't," she went on. "Not this. Dilly can come and go as she wishes. She's not a prisoner. She could go to the police any time the notion seized her."

"Like now."

"No. I told her that I would discuss the best thing for her to do with you, because you knew all about this sort of thing, who to see and all that. She agreed to wait until I had your opinion. She will."

"Are you asking for my opinion?"

"No. I want you to find whoever it was who killed that man. Then she would not need to become involved."

"That's police work, Mary. They have the resources to undertake homicide investigations. They have the ballistics lab, the fingerprint people, the forensic doctors, and the manpower to question a hundred people who might have seen or heard anything where he was killed."

"And with all of that do they always catch all the people who commit murder?"

I had to admit that the cops had a less than perfect success rate, and it was considerably less than perfect when they had no eyewitnesses or obvious motive, such as jealous spouse or rejected lover.

"All right," I said. "Granted. But asking me to do what the police haven't done so far may come out to nothing."

"Do I have another choice?"

"Get a lawyer and let him take Dilly in to tell her story."

"And what do you think will happen if she goes in and says that she killed Ted Fromann?"

My problem at that moment was that I didn't *know* what would happen. Normally the police would try to establish whether the confession merited further inquiry. People with a history of mental illness do confess to bizarre murders without any foundation. The police can't ignore such confessions, but they can't spend a lot of time on them either.

Paddock was the unknown factor. He might have taken a disliking to me, and the ACLU might disapprove of his methods, but so far as I knew he was an intelligent cop. What I didn't know was how badly he would want to close the file on Fromann. If he wanted it badly enough, he could make Daffodil Salamonica fit the bill and possibly settle for a plea of not guilty by reason of insanity. And then Dilly, sweet and otherworldly, the girl with the inner glow, would end up in St. E's, probably for the rest of her life.

98

I told Mary what should happen, and then I told her what could happen.

Mary closed her eyes tightly. She opened them and looked at me. "Do you want to tell me how stupid I was all these years? It wouldn't have come to this if I had just leveled with my folks and taken Dilly home and tried to get her some honest-to-God care in the bosom of her family."

"You did the best you could, Mary. You did what you thought was best for everybody."

"If I can get her through this, Cronyn, I'll take her home. Will you help her?"

"Mary, I . . . ," I started to say that she shouldn't pin any hopes on my efforts, that chances were slim to nonexistent I could turn up a killer out of the two million people, more or less, who live in Washington and its suburbs. I started to tell her about the problems and I saw that she didn't care about the problems. She wanted me to find Ted Fromann's killer.

So what I said was, "I'll have a go at it."

"What do you want me to do?"

"Tell me what you know about Dilly's involvement with Fromann."

She took a deep breath. "Nothing more than you already know. She became acquainted with him as a result of her . . . her affair with Katrina Onders. Trina was the only one she was close to." She hesitated as though remembering something.

"What is it, Mary?"

"The night before that house blew up, Dilly and Trina had a spat. Trina was supposed to spend the night with Dilly but, because of their argument, Trina went back to the house."

"Dilly never stayed in that house?"

"She told me once that no one ever did. Dilly told me she didn't even know Trina was part of a bomb group, or that they kept explosives in the house. The only hint she ever had was that Trina occasionally would cry out in the night that she was going to die, and Dilly would comfort her."

"The house was a bomb factory," I told her.

She nodded. "I had to go back to the old newspapers and the FBI and get whatever facts I could for Dilly's psychiatrist. He had to be able to separate Dilly's imaginings from reality.

"All four of them were in the house the morning of the explosion. The investigation confirmed that without a doubt. My sister called Trina that morning, early, to make up. The other girl, Jenny Whalen, answered the phone and brought Trina to it. Dilly and Trina talked for a long time, for so long, in fact, that one of the others, Mike Bristol, became angry. He was expecting a call, and Trina had kept the phone tied up for much longer than she should have. He insisted that she get off the phone. She and my sister talked for a few more minutes. They were in the middle of arranging to meet when the phone went dead. Dilly thought that Bristol had done something to it to get Trina off the line. It was later that she found out about the explosion. The county psychiatrist can explain why Dilly thinks she's responsible, but he can't do anything about it."

"Okay. The guilt she feels over Trina Onders' death is understandable. But over Fromann's? It doesn't make sense. Why should she feel any guilt over that? What could have happened between them that would have made her feel that way?"

Mary shook her head helplessly. "She won't talk to me about it, other than what I have already told you. All she says is that only the dead are permitted to know the secrets of the dead."

"Meaning that it's dangerous to know."

"I don't know. Maybe. Oh God, I don't know anything

anymore," she replied, pain and frustration in her voice. "She's slipping away, and I don't know what to do about it." Mary looked away. I gave her a moment or two of lip biting, waiting for her to come back to me. She did. "She never hurt anybody. She couldn't. All she ever wanted was for the world to be at peace and to be full of kindness and love. Other people gave her dope and told her that was the way to peace and love. Other people used her in their political crusades, people like you, Cronyn. You used my sister and others like her as cannon fodder in a cause she never understood. Take, take, take, that's all it was, and she gave until she hadn't anything left but a dream world."

She bit her lip some more, but it wasn't enough. She got to her feet and walked stiffly to the window and stared out, her fists clenching and unclenching. "She's imagining that she caused his death," Mary said in a broken voice. "I can't take that to the police. What chance would she have?"

"I'll do what I can," I said. "Knowing who killed Fromann might not help her."

She turned back to me, determination in her face. "Will not knowing?"

10

CARLOS RAMIREZ JUST dropped in, a little after four, coming from, he said, a meeting on the Hill with some congressmen concerned with the coffee question. He made a stab at explaining it, but I was more interested in why he came to see me.

"Over a drink," he suggested. "I'll buy."

I accepted, on the basis that we take turns, and went down to the street. His chauffeur waited there with a black Olds sedan that blocked half the street and drew irate honks and looks from the other drivers creeping by. The chauffeur, protected by the absolute immunity granted to his magic red, white, and blue license plates, looked totally unconcerned. He opened the rear door for me.

When I hesitated, Ramirez's smile faded. I supposed that he thought we would have an unseemly Alphonse and Gaston act there on the busy sidewalk. "Let's walk," I said to him.

He agreed, and we did the two blocks to the Hotel Washington briskly.

The lounge was a quietly lit place with dark wood on the walls and carpet on the floor. Two of the half-dozen or so tables were occupied. Three men in vested suits sat at one, talking among themselves over martinis. At the other, a man with wavy, gray hair smiled and hung on every word uttered by the earnest-looking young woman wearing a severely cut charcoal suit sitting next to him.

Ramirez and I took a corner table and ordered Manhattans.

"Have you found the letters you were looking for?" Ramirez asked.

"No. Why do you ask, Mr. Ramirez?"

"Carlos," he said. "Would you believe curiosity?"

I shook my head while the waitress put our drinks down and radiated in the brilliance of Ramirez's smile.

"Turn if off, Carlos," I said.

"Can't help it," he said, probably truthfully. "What's your first name?"

"Cronyn will do."

"Okay, Cronyn. It's like this. The more you have to poke around looking for those letters, the more chance someone else will find out about me and Mrs. D."

"That someone being your wife," I suggested. "I thought that sort of thing went unnoticed where you come from."

"Sure. Don't I wish. Women are the same everywhere, my friend, when they have the upper hand."

I refrained from suggesting that if anyone knew about that it should be him. Instead I offered this: "I thought they always had the upper hand."

He gave me that big grin. "I meant financially."

"Ah."

The grin faded. He slid his drink around the table, making little ellipses on its surface.

"When I was a kid," he said, "my father had to go into exile. I think he liked it. He put my mother up in comfortable middle-class circumstances in Boston with two of his unmarried sisters to keep their eyes on her while he spent most of his time and money in Europe. I went to school and college in the States. I've lived most of my life here." He gave some time to a private thought. It must have been a pleasant one because it brought a small smile to his face.

"I played a season of minor-league baseball," he said, after a moment, expressing the thought. It's odd that it should be so, but most men are impressed by something like that. A guy who is good enough to get paid for playing a kid's game has instant status, be he liar, cheat, drunk or whatever.

"I told my mother that the university debating team was going on tour," Ramirez went on. "It explained why I was going to places like Charlotte and Greensboro. My playing any sport professionally would have humiliated her." He hesitated. A look of sheer pleasure crossed his face. "It was the greatest five months in my life," he said.

"What did she say when she found out?" I asked.

"Nobody knows," he replied, grinning again. "I've never told anyone."

"Why tell me?"

"I don't know," he said. "I suppose I thought that you'd understand."

I didn't know what it was that he wanted me to understand, so I didn't say anything.

He swallowed some of his drink and expelled a deep breath. "Anyway," he resumed, looking at me. "My father left my mother just enough to keep her. I had to look out for myself."

"And so you married well."

"Yes. Maria's family has money and contacts. I depend upon her not only for my style of living but also for my job. That's how a guy with zero diplomatic experience becomes the number-three boy in the largest embassy my country maintains anywhere. I wouldn't last a minute if her uncles pulled the chain on me."

"Too bad. Some people I've talked to say you do a good job for your country."

"I do the best I can. We're a small country, Cronyn. We have a lot of poor people and more than enough diplomats. What we need is friends. I try to make them where I can. That's all."

I saw no point in telling him that, if friends were what his country needed, they'd sent the right guy.

I changed the subject. "The reason I haven't found the letters is that someone sent them to Paula Devlin, and she burned them." I waited for a response and received none. "You knew about that."

He shrugged. "Something."

"You had two ways of knowing," I suggested. "One is that she told you what happened."

"And the other way?" he asked.

"That you are the person who sent the letters to her."

He shook his head. "Huh-uh," he said. "I'd have never known about the letters but for your telling me."

"Then she told you that she burned them."

"She told me that you would probably cook up some story about the letters being destroyed."

"She did, did she? Whatever for?"

"She told me," said Ramirez, "that you would have to have a story to cover up your lie about her having written those letters. Especially, according to her, because you had failed to turn them up."

"But why would she tell you anything at all about them?" I thought I already had the answer to my own question, so I supplied it without waiting for him. "You went to her first and told her that I had questioned you at the embassy."

"Yes. I had only your word about those letters. I started to think about it later. You could have been trying to pull something."

"What did she tell you when you asked?"

"She said that she didn't know you and didn't know what you were up to but that she was certainly going to find out." He looked directly at me. "Are you on the level, Cronyn?"

"Yes."

He looked at me intently. "I think you are telling me the truth," he said.

"If I am, where does that leave Mrs. Devlin?"

He grinned. "She's a beautiful liar."

"Does that mean that she is a beautiful woman who lies or that she is a woman who lies beautifully?"

The grin broadened. "Either way," he said.

"But you believed her first, when she said there were no letters."

"Yes." The grin faded. "I know her fairly well, Cronyn. It was hard to believe that she would so far lose her restraint."

"With someone other than you, you mean."

He grunted a self-deprecating laugh and looked into his drink. "Yeah. Maybe that's it. Still . . . ," he looked up and moved the subject away from his own ego. "Whichever it is, if the letters no longer exist, there isn't anything for you to look for, and you're off the case."

"Would that make you happy?"

"Sure. It ought to make you happy, too. It ought to make everybody happy. Paula's off the hook. I don't need to worry about your turning up something on me that my wife won't like. You can find a paying client."

"Right. Everybody's happy. Except the cops. They have a body, and they want to know who handed it to them."

"The murder wasn't your problem the other night."

"That's what I said," I replied. "Then."

"I see," he said. "And now you're looking for the killer. Where do you start?"

"With you."

"Me?" He grinned. "I've been accused of a lot of things but never of murder."

"There's always a first time." I pushed my chair back. "You can tell Mrs. Devlin that you have accomplished your mission."

His grin faded. "Mission?"

"Oh, hell, Carlos. She asked you to see me and let her know for sure that I had swallowed her story about

107

burning the letters, didn't she?" I stood up. His silence was as good as an answer.

I went on. "I can understand her wanting me to drop the whole thing. She might even have made up the story of burning them, just so that I'd let her alone. What I don't understand is why you're so anxious. You know and I know that Paula Devlin didn't say anything about you in her letters to Fromann. We also both know that you're home free on your affair with Mrs. Devlin. So what worries you, Carlos?"

He looked away, not answering.

Annoyance crept up on me unawares, the kind of annoyance you feel when somebody you like is trying to con you.

"Thanks for the drink," I said and turned and walked away. At the door I looked back at him.

He sat alone, eyes down, making small, wet ellipses on the table with his glass. For someone who could make friends as easily as he did, he looked like the loneliest guy in the world.

The young blond woman came into the room and looked around. She tossed the cylindrical nylon bag she carried onto the dresser.

Her hair hung to her shoulders. She had a wide mouth and a beakish nose that could have used work, but she was not unattractive.

"Hi, Jack," she greeted me. "I'm Sissy."

"Hi, Sissy."

"Should've turned up the heat, Jack," she said over her shoulder to me. She unzipped the bag and showed me the gauzy pink smock she took from it. "This don't keep me too warm, honey."

She took off her leather-look jacket and started to unzip the fly of her leather-look pants, which clung to her shapely legs and buttocks. Sissy was a sprightly little

108

thing, despite being Jacquie Germaine's senior masseuse. When I called the number in the Yellow Pages, I had specified Jacquie's most experienced girl. The one who'd been around the longest was the one most likely to have known Carlos Ramirez. And the one most likely to know Ramirez was also the one most likely to know what he had been doing at the Just Heavenly about the time Ted Fromann entertained his killer.

I didn't doubt that Carlos Ramirez had a normally active libido. I wouldn't question his wife's suspicion that he had a mistress back at the ranch. What I couldn't see happening was Carlos paying for more. In fact I couldn't see Carlos paying for what he could get oodles of for free. So he had to have visited Jacquie Germaine's establishment for another reason.

Just because I had struck out on the hit-man theory with Jacquie didn't mean it was a loser. Jacquie was a smart woman, a survivor. She wouldn't give away the store in a moment of weakness or unexplained imbecility.

One of her girls might, especially if she didn't know all the implications of what she was telling me.

Sissy grinned, got rid of a wad of bubble gum from her mouth, and sat down on the edge of the bed. It was a standard motel bed in a standard motel on the Virginia side of the Potomac River.

She leaned back on her hands, her arms stiff behind her. Her breasts rose provocatively. "Like what you see, honey?" Her voice had a mountain twang to it. She launched into the various services that she could provide and the scale of prices.

"It's best just to go with it, honey," she assured me. She stroked her crotch. "Just go with the flow," she said soothingly, "and see what comes up."

It sounded not much different from going into a men's store for a necktie and coming out with a full suit of clothes. It makes you feel so good, you just don't know when to stop.

She started taking off her clothes.

"Don't bother," I said. "What I want is information."

She didn't like it, and she told me so. She stuffed the flimsy pink smock back into her bag.

"Sit down, Sissy. I'm not kidding around."

"Don't get tough with me, Jack."

"I'll get as tough as I have to."

She went for the bag again. I grabbed her wrist before she got to it. I twisted her back onto the bed. Her eyes looked scared, but her voice was still defiant. "Is this how you get your kicks?"

I picked up the bag with one hand and shook it empty. Its contents made a little pile on the bed beside us. The item that interested me most of all was a little twenty-five-caliber automatic. I stuck my index finger through the trigger guard and held it up before her.

"Got a license?" I asked.

"A girl has to protect herself from creeps like you," she answered me.

I ignored her complaint. "What do you know about Carlos Ramirez?"

"Let me out of here before I start screaming my head off," she warned.

"Sure." I let her up and pointed toward a chair in the corner. "Go sit and tell me about Carlos."

She picked herself up from the bed and went to the chair in the corner and sat. Her eyes flicked to the pile on the bed, "Hurry up," she said.

"Ramirez came to your place on Monday. You'd know him. Good-looking guy. Wears expensive clothes." I searched my mind for another way to jog her memory. Airports came to mind. "He's probably carrying a suitcase, since he just got off a plane."

"Don't know him," she replied. "I gotta split."

"Huh-uh, Sissy. What you gotta do is talk to me about Carlos Ramirez. If you don't, I pick up the phone and call an Arlington cop and I show him your work clothes and the gun and say you tried to roll me, or something like that. Bad news any way you look at it, Sissy."

Her eyes, scared, turned toward the pile on the bed. "No cops," she said. Her voice sounded strained, as though her mouth had suddenly gone dry. She looked back to me. "I'll tell you what I can, only no cops. Unnerstand?"

"Deal," I assured her. "You know him?"

"I don't know him, but I've seen him a couple of times," she admitted. "Not Monday, though. I wasn't there."

"Ever take care of him?"

"No."

"Does he have a favorite girl?"

She thought about that for half a second. "Jacquie, maybe."

"Jacquie?"

She shrugged at my astonishment. "They go into her office together," she said. "I've seen it. And of course the other girls have too. You have to wonder. A good-looking guy like that. But I've seen stranger ways of gettin' it off." She hesitated. "Course, I don't know what they do in there. He usually stays ten, maybe fifteen minutes and then he's gone."

"Many customers come to see Jacquie?"

"Are you kidding? In that dump? It's an outcall business." Her glance returned to the bed. "Can I git my stuff together?" she asked.

"In a minute," I said. I twirled the automatic around my finger and smiled at her. "Know many guys who use these?"

Her face held a blank look. "What?"

"Some people shoot other people as a business, only

they can't advertise. They have to have a contact point, where the buyer of the service and the seller get together or work through a middleman. Or middlewoman, in Jacquie's case."

Her eyes looked startled. "Jacquie? Your flag's stuck halfway up the pole, Jack," she informed me with certainty. "Jacquie never goes into anything where she doesn't see a chance of talking herself out of it."

I persisted and got nowhere with the contract killer idea. The hell of it was that I was glad that I hadn't. Something inside me didn't want Carlos Ramirez to be guilty of killing Ted Fromann, at least not that way, not cold-bloodedly, using a paid killer. If he did do it, I wanted him to have shot Fromann in a Latin passion, protecting the reputation of the woman he loved. Maybe he saw something in her that was worth it that I would never see.

I sighed, gave the gun another twirl, and dropped it on the bed casually beside the pile.

Sissy's eyes narrowed and she wet her lips with her tongue. She watched warily as I stood by her belongings. "It's just girl stuff," she said, offering an explanation where none had been asked for.

I scanned the objects of her explanation, as though I hadn't noticed them before. "What? Oh, sure, Sissy," I agreed. The pile contained the gauzy smock, on the bottom now because it had been on the top of the bag. Spread in disarray over it were various creams and jellies, some panties, a paperback romantic novel, and at least one disposable douche. Odds and ends of girl stuff, except for one thing that had slid from the top of the pile and lay hidden from Sissy's view along the side. Three things, actually, held together by a paper clip.

She spoke again, her voice insistent in her anxiety to draw my attention away from the bed. "Who is this guy Ramirez? What's the beef against him?"

I turned to her and gave her a smile. "Wife trouble," I said. "Ramirez had a girlfriend. Wife doesn't like that but his using Jacquie's services is the last straw for her."

"She must be something to look at if she's worried about Jacquie." She started to stand up. "I gotta go," she said. "If I take too long without anything to show for it, Jacquie'll think I'm knocking down."

I took three twenties from my wallet and handed them to her. Surprise showed in her face. "You've earned it," I said. "Sorry if I scared you."

"That's okay," she said quickly.

"What do you suppose Jacquie and Carlos do in that room alone?" I asked.

She palmed her twenties and fidgeted. "Damned if I know. Maybe they say a prayer together. Jacquie's a big one for religion, you know. Goes to church every day to pray."

"Yeah," I said. "See you around, Sissy."

I went out of the room. Behind me, Sissy hurried toward the bed, either to retrieve her pistol or those three tiny, clear plastic pouches with the white powder inside. The last look on her face told me she would sooner meet a case of the flu than me again.

11

A YOUNG RED-HAIRED guy crossed the carpeted floor of Walter Devlin's outer office. He gave the appearance of heading me off, but that was just show for the secretary's sake. He had, the instant after he started to move, looked into my eyes, and the fight had gone out of him. I saw it but the secretary didn't, and I saw no point in rubbing Red's face in his fear. I moved fast enough to make it look like a real race. You could almost see the relief in his eyes when I beat him to Devlin's door.

I opened it, went in, and shut it behind me. "You're Walter Devlin?" I said to the man behind the chrome-and-glass desk that filled the floor space in front of a broad window. The window overlooked Connecticut Avenue from eight stories up. No traffic noise penetrated its quiet solitude.

As I crossed the room to the desk, my feet sank into a thick, beige carpet that matched the soft plush of the deep chairs. Oriental silk-screen prints hung on the walls under glass. A soft glow of diffused light enveloped the room from the ceiling. A mirrored cabinet, probably a bar, stood in the corner. In the other, three more of those cuddly, beige chairs clustered around a tile-topped table.

"Who are you?" Devlin stood up. His hand reached for the telephone, fingers groping for the proper button to summon either his secretary or Red, the young assistant. The only other objects on the glass surface of the desk were a silver cigarette box and silver ashtray, a pen set with a green malachite base, a clock and calendar to match, and a leather folio, which Devlin closed as I approached.

He was a small, trim man whose tailored blue suit fit him without an obvious wrinkle. His silver-gray hair was thinner than it had once been, probably, but still adequate to cover his head. He had high cheekbones, tapering to a narrow chin.

"Dan Cronyn," I replied.

His eyes flicked momentarily toward the door. "I don't recall seeing your name on my appointment list."

The door opened behind me. I stood aside and turned to keep both Devlin and the door in view. Red might have found a helper.

The secretary, pale of face, appeared in the doorway. "I'm sorry, Mr. Devlin. He just barged through."

"I tried," I told him. "I called yesterday for an appointment and again this morning. I was polite to her both times and told her that it was important. She's very protective."

He waved her out with an annoyed gesture. He looked like a hard man to work for. If you want tolerance for your occasional lapses, be sure not to apply for a job with Walter Devlin.

He sat down in a high-backed swivel chair behind the desk. He put the tips of his fingers together and rolled them toward me.

"Well?" he said. "Please be as concise as possible. I have a full schedule today."

I walked to one of the chairs facing the desk, rearranged it so I could see the door out of the corner of my eye, and sat down. "I'm a private investigator. A man named Fromann, who also went by the name of Atwood, was murdered on Monday. I'd like to know who did it."

"What does that have to do with me?"

"You're a suspect."

"By whose reckoning?"

"Mine."

"All right, Cronyn. You've had your minute. Beat it."

"Talk to me or to the cops," I told him. "One way or another, I'll get what I came for." It was a bluff but he couldn't know that. On the other hand, I had no way of knowing whether he'd mind talking to the cops. The basis for the bluff lay in my assumption that Devlin, with his background, would want to avoid the police if possible.

He thought about it while he took a cigarette from a gold case and fitted it to a silver holder. Before he lit it, he looked back to me. "What assurance do I have that you won't drag the police into my affairs even if I do talk to you?"

"None," I told him. "If you don't talk to me, you will for sure talk to the cops. If you do talk to me, you may not have to talk to the cops. It's just a case of the odds."

"I'll give you a few more minutes."

"Where were you Monday afternoon between twelve and three?"

He smiled, but the smile had no warmth in it. He leaned forward and pulled an appointment book toward him and consulted it. "Lunch with a business associate and then back to the office for appointments," he told me.

"Can your business associate confirm it?"

"If necessary. I believe that I also have a credit card charge slip," he replied.

"You paid for lunch?"

"I usually do."

"And you came directly back to the office?"

"That's right. My secretary and my assistant can confirm it."

"I'll bet that they'd lie for you."

"I'd expect they would if they wanted to keep their jobs. In this case, however, it's not necessary." He lit his

117

cigarette and leaned back in the chair and considered me thoughtfully. "Who are you working for, Cronyn?"

"The way it's supposed to work in these things is that I ask the questions."

He ignored my statement. "Is it my wife?"

"Why would you think that, Mr. Devlin?"

"She came to your office the other day, I'm told."

"Someone told me that, too," I said. "That someone goes by the name of Taffy. You know him?"

Devlin expelled smoke toward the ceiling. An air-conditioning vent sucked it out of the room. Nice.

He spoke. "Taffy is a very close associate."

"I guess that means he works for you," I said. The only response to that was a slight tilt of his head. I went on. "There's only one reason a man would have his wife followed. He suspects her of an affair. Now that could give you a motive for murder."

He tapped ash from the end of his cigarette. "You made two errors, Cronyn. First, Taffy was not following my wife. He had some shopping to do downtown. He happened to see her and tried to catch up to her, without success. Second, Paula is not having an affair. She's much too devoted to me." He smiled again, coldly, a cynical curling of the corners of his mouth. "She's also far too clever to be caught."

So Taffy had lied to his boss about following Mrs. Devlin. I wondered why. I also wondered why Devlin had pretended not to know me when I arrived, so I asked him about that.

"Since Taffy told you about me, you had to know who I was when I came in here," I pointed out.

He blew more smoke toward the ceiling. "What's your game, Cronyn?"

"No game," I assured him. "I have a client who could get into trouble as a consequence of Fromann's murder. The only way to keep that from happening is to find the killer."

118

Devlin took extreme care removing his half-burned cigarette from his holder and snuffing it out in his ashtray. For a long moment he did not look at me. Even when he spoke, his gaze remained fixed on the stirring around he was doing in his ashtray. "Tell me, Cronyn, do you think your investigation is likely to be a lengthy one?"

"Hopefully not."

"I see. I gather your client hasn't the resources for a sustained search for that man's murderer. Therefore I see our interests merging."

"Tell me about it."

"If you continue to go about asking embarrassing questions, you could, inadvertently of course, break a great deal of china in the fragile world of business. That could cost me some money. Naturally the prospect doesn't please me." He paused to make sure I was getting the picture.

When he saw the light on my face, he went on. "On your part, you too stand to lose money, if your client cannot recompense your efforts. I have a solution." He seemed pleased with himself.

"I'd like to hear it."

"I would like to hire you. It would be necessary for you to go out of town, on expenses, of course, say for two weeks. Let's see, Miami Beach is delightful at this time of the year. That would be just about right, wouldn't you say? Two weeks in the Fountainbleau or the Eden Roc?"

"I don't think I could catch up to Ted Fromann's killer in Miami Beach," I said.

"I don't think you would care," he said. "I have old friends in Miami. I could ask them to be sure you did not become lonely."

I stood up. "Thanks, Mr. Devlin. You're more than generous, and I'm sorry I might get in the way around here, but I already have a job and a client." I walked to his desk and laid my card on it. "If you think of anything that will help, call me."

His jaw set and his eyes turned hard. "Don't meddle in things you don't understand," he said. It sounded like a warning.

I started out of the room, thought of something, and turned back. "You didn't mention the restaurant where you had lunch."

"I want to cooperate, Cronyn. In return, I hope that you stay out of my affairs. The restaurant was the Old Europe."

I knew the restaurant. Not Devlin's style. "The Old Europe? I'd have expected something more like the Lion d'Or or Dominique's."

"My guest didn't want to be seen in the usual places. It happens sometimes."

"I'm sure it does. In case you didn't know it, the Old Europe is less than five minutes from the scene of the murder."

"I didn't know it," he said, his voice flat.

"So long, Mr. Devlin."

I walked back to the office from Devlin's Connecticut Avenue address, a cold drizzle settling around my head and neck. It made Devlin's offer of two weeks in Miami Beach sound appealing. I tried to add up the cost to him of an eighty-hour fee, plus expenses in a hundred-and-fifty-dollar-a-day hotel. I lost the subtotal as I got to figuring how many nine-dollar hamburgers I could eat and how many five-dollar martinis I could drink in two weeks.

Whatever it came to, it was plenty, and I doubted that I was worth it. So far as I could see, I wasn't a threat to anyone. After all, my investigation so far had turned up no one who admitted knowing either Fromann or about the letters. And without that admission, or proof of the lie which hid it, I had no suspects, only suspicions.

120

A metropolitan police cruiser stood at the curb in front of my building. Inside the lobby, a uniformed officer wearing a fur-collared jacket talked to Ralph. She wore no cap. Her hair was black and twisted up around her head.

Ralph saw me and said something to the cop. She walked over to me. "Mr. Cronyn?" she asked. Her tone was polite. I admitted to being Mr. Cronyn, and she said, "Detective Paddock wishes to see you."

"Am I under arrest?"

"That's one alternative," said the cop evenly.

"What's the other?"

"Detective Paddock would like to talk to you informally at the scene of the Fromann murder. He said that something had occurred to him and you might be able to help out with some details."

"Otherwise?"

"I'll have to take you into custody," she said, "as a material witness."

I looked at her. She weighed possibly a hundred-fifteen, about eighty-five pounds under the least that I could hope to come in at. Not even her gun could have helped her in a contest of physical mastery.

It was her badge that did it. It had as much authority behind it as the ones worn by cops twice her size.

I sighed. "Always ready to give Detective Paddock the benefit of my analysis," I told her, and we went out to the cruiser.

When we arrived at the Northwest Gardens, she waited in the car. I went up to the late Ted Fromann's apartment. The door was locked. Paddock opened it in response to my knock and invited me in.

He had taken off his raincoat. He wore a well-used corduroy sport jacket. His tie was pulled away from his neck. His black eyes revealed nothing. He said, "Wait a

121

minute," as I started down the short hall to the living room. "I want you to see this," he added as he stood there holding the door.

He released the door. It swung closed, the latch bolt sliding home in the door frame with an audible click. He tugged on the knob without turning it. The door was solidly closed.

"That's the fourteenth time this afternoon I've done that," he said. "Closes every time. Curious how it just happened to be open on the day you found Fromann's body, isn't it? You did say that, didn't you? That the door was open?"

"Let me try it," I said.

He stood aside. I turned the knob and pulled the door inward. Instead of letting it swing shut from the open position, I closed it gently and prevented the latch bolt from engaging. I stepped back.

"Like that," I said.

"Deliberately left ajar?" he asked, skeptical.

"If that's the only way."

"Sure." Paddock pushed the door shut and walked on into the living room and sat down on a straight chair at the end of the coffee table. At the other end stood the armchair. He nodded toward it. "Have a seat." It was the only other place to sit in the room. The couch had disappeared, probably to the police laboratory, leaving a conspicuous gap. In the wall behind where the couch had stood were two holes in the plaster.

Paddock saw the direction of my glance. "Two of the slugs went through Fromann and the back of the couch," he explained.

"So I guessed," I said and sat down in the armchair. "They call this police harassment," I went on, looking at him.

"The fuck they do," he said, his voice attempting a tone of mock surprise. "The way I look at it, I'm doing you a favor. I bring you out here so you don't have to make a trip down to Indiana Avenue to carry those letters to me."

I didn't say anything.

He waited for a reply. When a few seconds had passed without getting it, he said, "Push is coming to shove, cowboy. You should have been out there looking for those letters. Instead you been cocking around Jacquie Germaine's whorehouse. Not smart, cowboy. Not smart at all."

He'd tell me, if he wanted to, how he had connected me with Jacquie Germaine. It would do no good to ask. "I had an itch that needed scratching," I said.

"I hear that Jacquie does business with some white guy. Not a customer. More like a partner. You?"

I shook my head. "You bucking for Vice?"

Paddock spread his lips flat across his teeth. It was a look that I didn't like because above the phony smile his eyes glinted in icy blackness. The look reminded me of the leader of a pack of wolves who had their prey cornered.

"Still an uptown smart-ass, eh cowboy?" he observed. He stood up, put his raincoat on, and turned the chair around so that, when he straddled it, he could rest his arms on the top of its back. "Now, let's go through it again. You came here to make a deal with Fromann over some letters. You found him dead. Lucky for you, three people saw you come into the building and fixed the time as upwards of an hour or more after the time of death."

"That's the way it happened," I said.

"No, here's the way it happened," he said, leaning forward, his head pushed over the back of the chair. "You kill Atwood and get out of here in a sweat. You're scared. But maybe you forget something, something that ties you to Fromann. You dream up that story and come back here, this time making sure that people see you."

"I was in my office," I told him, "when Fromann got it."

"Anyone who can confirm it?"

"I made a few phone calls."

"You could have done that from anywhere and told the person on the other end that you were calling from your office."

"Except I didn't. I had an appointment with the woman who wrote the letters. I was waiting for her." I paused. "In my office. That's a half-hour from here at that time of the afternoon. Try it sometime."

His mouth worked silently. "Sure," he said, after a long moment of silence. "The letters. The woman. All right, smart-ass. As of this moment you need an alibi in a case of murder."

I was beginning not to like this. The man seemed serious. He was measuring me for a suit of prison denims. The police don't dispassionately weigh all the evidence in a murder. They look around for the most likely suspect and begin to gather evidence on that individual. I didn't care for the honor.

At that point, I considered telling him that the woman's name was Paula Devlin and that she had destroyed her letters. Something kept me from doing it; something inside the cold shell that surrounded my brain told me I had said too much already.

"If I'm in custody, Paddock, I want a lawyer. If I'm not in custody, I've got other things to do." I stirred in my chair to give him the idea that I was leaving.

He unbuttoned the jacket beneath the raincoat. "You'll go when I tell you to go."

Somewhere under there was a three fifty-seven magnum, probably. I didn't have to see it to know it was there. He wasn't going to shoot me, I was sure of that, but you have to have a better reason for risking the wrath of a man with a gun than his violation of your civil rights. I stopped stirring in my chair.

"You made up the story of the letters," he went on. "Those letters never existed."

"You have to do better than that, Paddock. What about a motive?"

"Yeah," he said. For a long moment of silence he looked at me across the coffee table. His head seemed to slide down into the collar of his raincoat. His black eyes, half-hooded, glittered. "I got an idea about that," he said finally. "I checked your record. Chicago confirms your arrest during that riot in 1968."

"I wasn't rioting," I corrected him. "The police were."

"Sure," said Paddock, eyes glittering. "And we had you cold for smoking pot on the steps of the Justice Department. Like you said, you had a friendly judge."

"That's ancient history."

"Is it?"

"You know it is. I'm surprised that anybody cares enough to keep the records. What about the FBI?"

"They're not talking," he replied, a little bitterly.

"That's nice," I said. "I'll remember that the next time I'm asked about my youthful transgressions."

"Yeah. Well, I figure that somebody who would burn buildings down or blow them up wouldn't mind pulling a trigger six times if he had to."

"You got the wrong boy," I told him. "I steered clear of those people. What's all this got to do with anything?"

"A lot of the worst of those radicals are still in hiding," he replied. "Some have come out in the open, but not the ones with the heavy trouble waiting for them. They'll never come out if they can help it."

"The so-called underground guerrilla movement," I said. "They're mostly mild-mannered accountants or bourgeois housewives now, approaching middle age under assumed names. Big deal."

"Some of them are looking at hard time if the Feds finger them. Maybe you're one of them. Maybe your record doesn't cover everything you did."

I stood up. "You're blowing smoke."

"Am I?" he said, looking up at me. His head and neck came out of his collar. "Take away those letters, cowboy, and look at what you have left. That you were at the scene of the crime. That you and Fromann were both into that radical crap years ago. That Fromann was getting money from somebody because he had something on that somebody. You are that somebody. When the price got too high you popped the sonofabitch right here, right in this goddamned room."

His voice had risen and so had he, off the seat of the chair by a couple of inches, his knees flexed. His black eyes glittered; his nostrils flared.

I started toward the door, my back to him. I heard him bark my name. I turned. He had stood up.

"I'll tell you one more thing, Paddock," I told him, "and then you can go to hell. I've been down that same road and there ain't nothing at the end of it, because of one simple fact. Fromann was on the run himself. He was the one facing the sure hard time, three and five, plus whatever they'd add on for running. No way was he going to turn himself in and have them lay that on him, not for anything he could tell about his old comrades."

He walked up to me. He was the shorter of us, but you could see the power in him. And you could feel something else, a spring wound too tightly, ready to let go. But that was his problem, not mine.

"Got all the answers," he said, his eyes no longer cold now but hot, a smoldering blackness reflecting an inner inferno. "Like any street punk, you got all the answers. You figure I'll walk you in and some uptown lawyer's

126

going to walk you out, laughing. Don't count on it, cowboy. I'm going to bust your ass, tomorrow, the day after, next week."

That's when I knew why I hadn't told him about Paula Devlin or about her burning the letters in the backyard of her half-million-dollar townhouse. If I had told Paddock, she'd have called me a liar, just as she'd promised to do. He'd believe her because he wanted to believe that I had made up the story to cover for my killing Fromann. Her lie would form the corroboration for his theory. But as long as he didn't know her, he didn't have that.

"No, you won't, Paddock. You know why? Because out there somewhere is a packet of hot letters and a woman who can say that she sent me to get them. You pull me in and that uptown lawyer will have you make your best case about Fromann and me and the old days and then, when you're way out on that limb, we spring the woman and the letters and you look like a fool. So go jerk off someplace else and let me alone."

I should have been watching for what happened next, but I wasn't. The movement of his arm registered on my mind, but it gave me no time to do anything about it. The blow probably traveled no more than ten inches but it felt as though it had started in Wisconsin. His fist hit me just above the belly-button and knocked my diaphragm out of sync. I tried gasping, but before anything came into my lungs, he hit me in the kidney at the same time he stuck out one foot in front of my ankle in order to help me toward the floor.

I sprawled just inside the living room, feeling as though I was going to throw up. He didn't give me any time to think about that.

Agony in my right knee. His shoe was hard, and I wondered momentarily if he wore factory shoes, the ones with steel toes.

I sensed him moving around me as I started to get up.

127

Agony in the other knee, then, and I slipped back to the floor, my cheek against the late Ted Fromann's cheap carpet.

"Damn shame about these slippery floors," said Paddock from above me. "Maybe you can sue the management. Meantime, cowboy, button up that smart-ass jive you're giving me. You're going down, either the easy way or the hard way. It's up to you. Think it over."

I was still trying to get up as he left. I crawled up a wall for support. The left knee wasn't too bad but the other one wasn't fit to stand on.

I swore aloud at the closed door. When I ran out of all the obscenities that came to mind, I repeated them.

I tried walking, not too successfully. The knees hurt. They'd get better, eventually. I wasn't so sure about my self-esteem, and in the flush of hot anger some of the pain disappeared, while I tried to convince myself that I had been very, very lucky.

If I had seen that punch coming a half-second earlier, I'd have had to answer to charges of assaulting a police officer. Of course, he could assault me, and that's all right because there were no witnesses and he'd left no serious injuries or marks that could not be explained by my unfortunate fall on a slippery floor.

His colleagues must know, I was sure, of Paddock's methods. True to the code, they'd say nothing. Maybe they'd even back him up if it came down to a formal hearing on a citizen's complaint. A few might even lie for him. He'd know who those few were. His partner for sure, maybe the girl cop who had brought me to him.

I was getting tired of feeling like the doormat after every meeting with Paddock, yet I had to admit that he was in the catbird seat, and there wasn't a hell of a lot I could do about it.

I tried swearing again, but my heart just wasn't in it by

then. The swearing ended with something like a sigh, and I limped out of Fromann's apartment in search of a cab, my only consolation the thought that I was in better shape than Fromann had been when he left there.

12

I CAUGHT UP to Taffy in a gym on Nebraska Avenue in far Northwest. It occupied, inconspicuously, a double unit in a row of small shops along a service road parallel to the Avenue. A discreet sign said "Jonathon's Gym and Health Club, Members Only."

After some explanations to a guy with thin, white hair and hostile eyes, I was allowed into the main salon to look for Taffy. I crossed the red-carpeted floor, surrounded by gleaming chrome contraptions designed for lifting, tugging, pushing, bending over, or running on, a tribute to the ingenuity of the human mind which, having invented machines to take all the physical labor out of life, has now invented machines to put it back. Mirrors surrounded me, mirrors that afforded the lifters, tuggers, pushers, benders and runners the opportunity to admire the results of their efforts, checking on pecs and glutes at the same time. The whole place reeked of modernity. efficiency, and sweat.

I located Taffy at the bench press, on his back in tight, tan shorts. He wore straps around his wrists and a headband across his forehead, restraining the flowing gold of his hair. Before I spoke to him, I mentally totaled up the weights ringing his bar and hoped he wouldn't make it. He clasped the bar, rotated his hands a little for the right grip, closed his eyes, and pushed. The veins in his neck stood out like hard cords. The bar rose and hung there until he let it drop back into its rest, expelling a satisfied grunt as he did so. He breathed heavily. A sheen of sweat made his hairless chest shine.

Next to us a man with dead-white skin and skinny legs peddled slowly on a stationary bicycle. His attention was focused more on Taffy than on the bike. He kept shooting sidelong glances toward the bench press.

"Hello, Taffy," I said.

His eyes rolled back to see me above and behind him. For a moment they showed anxiety, almost fear, then he smiled and said, "Hello, turkey. Want to give it a push?"

"Not today," I said.

He giggled and slid off the bench. The middle-aged guy on the bike stared. Taffy deliberately ran his forefinger slowly up his own sternum. The guy's eyes started to bulge, and Taffy chose that moment to turn in the man's direction. The man turned hastily away, his face reddening.

"What are you staring at?" asked Taffy, accusingly.

The man mumbled something and crawled off the bike and headed, shoulders hunched and eyes down, out of the room.

"You're such a nice guy, Taffy," I said. "A prince."

He grinned at me, a smug, self-satisfied grin. "He had his fantasy," he said. "Whaddya want, Cronyn? Another shot at me?"

"Sometime," I answered. "Just now talk is enough."

"Okay," he said and led me into the lounge, where he poured himself a glass of vegetable juice out of a pitcher from a yellow refrigerator. We sat on chrome-and-plastic chairs around a square formica-topped table, also yellow. "So talk."

"You have a problem," I informed him.

He stared at me. Then he laughed. "I have a problem?" He laughed. "Get lost, turkey."

"Maybe you can't see it, but it's there."

His eyes, tinted with suspicion, considered me. "You're no problem, Cronyn. I can take you."

"I didn't say that I was your problem."

132

He drank some of his vegetable juice and wiped his mouth with the back of his bare arm. "Tell me about my problem. Who is it? I'd like to meet the guy that I can't take."

I wanted to tell him that he would, someday, because when you go around with the attitude that you're the best, you always find somebody who's better. I wanted to tell him, but I didn't. I hadn't come for an unwinnable argument on who was the strongest in the land. His magic mirrors in the other room had already convinced him that he was. That, plus all those steel saucers he'd been pushing toward the mirrored ceiling when I came in.

"Your problem is either your boss or your boss's wife," I told him. "Maybe both."

His eyes narrowed a little, but he kept his mouth shut, waiting for me to say more.

I did. "Walter Devlin, Taffy. I see you having this problem with Devlin because of his wife. You want to get her out of the way but you can't figure out how to do it. She made you look like a jerk kid once, because she's smarter than you."

His pretty face reddened and the corners of his mouth turned down. "Watch it, turkey," he said.

"What you needed," I went on, ignoring the implied threat, "was a sure thing. You could spend the rest of your life trying to catch her in something and wind up having your own can booted out instead of hers."

"Bullshit, Cronyn. Walter wouldn't let me go."

"He would if you kept harassing him with hysterical accusations about his wife. I think that Devlin knows your limits, Taffy, and is satisfied with them. But he doesn't suffer fools, and one more time like the last time and out you go. Be tough to go back to hustling one-night stands again after you got it made with Devlin. Really tough."

He smiled at me then, a loose and easy smile. "You want to go to the hospital, Cronyn? Last time I was nice to you because the guy in the lobby could have caused trouble for me. But this isn't like the last time. I don't have to be nice to you because nobody here will come down on me for protecting myself against some used-up private cop."

"You're right," I agreed. "This isn't like the last time." I eased forward slightly and pulled my feet back, getting them under my center of gravity. I put my left hand under the table, assuming that if he wanted to make good on his offer he'd start with shoving the table toward me. The left hand was to guide it and me in different directions so that I could slide off to my right. "This time, darling, we start even."

A silence came over us, a silence underlined by the usually unnoticed sound of the refrigerator kicking on with a click and a hum. The smile slowly faded from Taffy's face as his brain worked through the situation.

Then he decided. On talk. "Don't push me," he said.

My legs and shoulders relaxed, shedding a tension I had not even been aware of. I had learned something about Taffy. He wouldn't come out of his corner unless he could see his edge. It was his survivor's instinct. I didn't want to think about what it would be like if you had to go in after him. Not nice. I remembered all those weights on his last press.

"Ever been to the Northwest Garden Apartments?" I asked. "They're three or four blocks west of Wisconsin."

He took another swallow of his health cocktail. "Maybe. Maybe not. Why?"

"A guy lived there under the name of Murray Atwood, real name Ted Fromann. Know him?"

"You ask a lot of questions, Cronyn. No reason I should answer."

"No reason you should sit here either, but you are. If

you weren't curious about me and where I'm coming from you'd be in the massage room."

He didn't want to admit his curiosity, so he didn't. He just sat there waiting for me to speak my piece.

"It's like this, Taffy, the more I think about the mess your boss's wife got herself into, the more I wonder how a guy like Fromann connected with her in the first place."

"At a bar?"

"She go to bars alone very often? You've had your eye on her, and remember, you can tell me the truth. I'm not Devlin. You might tell him she hangs out in bars all the time, whether it's true or not. You have to tell me the truth or you'll never see where I'm headed."

He thought it over. "All right," he said. "No bars. How then?"

"First you have to understand Fromann's situation. He was up against it, living in a horse barn in Virginia, bumming what he could get from old buddies, using another name because he was wanted by the FBI. Where does his world intersect with hers? She's the good-looking wife of a well-to-do businessman. She lives in a five-hundred-thousand-dollar townhouse in Georgetown. She's a woman whose goal in life it is to impress her husband's clients with her genteel sophistication, a woman who shops only in the quality stores, and dines only in the most elegant restaurants, a woman who knows what plays are in and what people are out."

Taffy almost ground his teeth. The muscles in his face tightened. Hell would have a hard freeze before he admitted Paula Devlin had any qualities useful to her husband. "What are you getting at, Cronyn?"

"This. Somebody had to steer Fromann to her. Out of several million people in D.C. and the suburbs, chances for an accidental meeting between those two were remote to the point of being nonexistent."

"You got somebody in mind?"

"Yes. Somebody who thought that, if she cheated on Devlin once, she'd do it again. Somebody who saw the chance to trap her in a love affair by setting her up, like he had tried to do once before. Only this time he'd be in control because he was paying Fromann to act the stud. She would not have the chance to make him look stupid again."

He reddened again. "Stupid?" he spat out. "Man, you're the one who's stupid. You *own* stupid. I never even heard of anybody named Fromann."

"And you never been to the Northwest Gardens. Tell me about it."

"All right. So I was there. I told you I followed her, for crissakes. But I didn't know which apartment she went into. How could I?"

I ignored his protest. "Where'd it go wrong? The letters? Fromann had the letters, and he saw where he could make a lot more from Paula Devlin than you could give him. You found out about the doublecross and killed him."

He stared at me. Then he pinched his lower lip between the thumb and forefinger of his right hand. I gave him all the time he needed to think over his reply to my accusation.

"What damn letters?" he said finally, his eyes blank.

He looked genuinely baffled, and Taffy just wasn't bright enough to pull that off so convincingly if he had known about the letters. I felt caught in that halfway world where the known facts contradict your theory yet you cling to it because it's all you have left. So I went on.

"She wrote intimate letters to him, and he wanted to sell them back to her—for a price, of course."

"You're kidding," he said, incredulous. It was an impressive display of innocence. It convinced me.

He went on, his mind digesting what I'd told him. "So Paula was sleeping with this guy," he said. "I'll be damned. Not only was she sleeping with the guy, but she also was writing him dirty letters." He rubbed his hands together, marking his deep satisfaction.

He looked at me, smiling. "Thanks, turkey. That puts me in the driver's seat."

I stood up. I had come to Taffy's gym with an idea, hoping to find a spot in the puzzle just made for the big blond. It hadn't worked out, and I had given away more than I'd received. Instead of connecting Taffy with Fromann's scheme to shakedown Paula Devlin, I had given to him freely what I had been at such pains to conceal on our first meeting. He was definitely a happy individual.

I looked down at him. "You like that, huh?"

He grinned back. "She's out, Cronyn. Finished."

"She's his wife," I replied. "Maybe he thinks he needs her."

"He wants a woman, he can have one of our party girls," said Taffy.

"There might be more to it than that. I hear that Devlin demands loyalty. The only way you get that is by returning it."

Taffy snorted. "He doesn't need her. He needs me. He knows that he can count on me."

"And when he doesn't need you anymore? What then, Taffy? Are you the disposable man, as she is the disposable woman?"

Taffy laughed at the notion. "I can handle myself, turkey. See how I got everything out of you I needed to know about her?"

He sounded cocky. He looked cocky. And there wasn't much I could do about it, or about him. I could give Paula Devlin a few days' breathing room, however; even though I wasn't sure I owed it to her.

"One thing," I said. "You think you have Paula Devlin over a barrel now. You don't. You can't use any of this that I told you because you can't back it up. To Devlin, it's just another example of your childish jealousy, probably the last he'll put up with."

"What about the letters?"

"They're gone. Try making him believe she wrote dirty letters to another man. *His* wife? Sort of a shame. You know everything you ever wanted to know about Paula and you can't tell Devlin anything about it, without making yourself look bad."

I turned away, leaving him sitting there with his pretty face blank as he tried to digest the futility of his situation. It would give him something to think about. He'd have to give his brain a workout, trying to come up with a way to let Devlin know about the faithless wife, without putting himself in the position of spiteful gossip.

Taffy had his problem, and I had mine. Dilly Salamonica sat waiting for an answer, sure I had it. In twenty years, nothing had changed. Except me. I no longer had the answer. Now all I had was the responsibility.

I sucked in the cold air outside the gym, savoring its freshness. Someone had pointed Ted Fromann in the direction of Paula Devlin. I needed to find out who.

Paula Devlin agreed, reluctantly, to talk to me, as she put it, "for the last time." She gave me a west Alexandria address where we could meet, so I headed for Virginia.

I accelerated the station wagon after leaving the confusion of lane-switching drivers on the 14th Street bridge and picked up speed southbound on Shirley Highway. To my left stood the high-rises of Crystal City and Pentagon City. On the right, the sand-colored stone mass of the Pentagon looked almost gray under the dull, gray sky of that dull, gray afternoon.

Fluorescent lights made cool, white rectangles of the windows. Only God and the Russians knew what the generals and admirals were up to behind those windows. I didn't want to know. To retain one's sanity in an insane

138

world, it's best not to know everything.

My tires slapped against the wet pavement as I eased the speed up to fifty. The windshield wipers repeated their muted squish-click, squish-click, all the way to Landmark. I parked in the shopping-center lot and walked to the apartment she'd told me to come to.

It was one of those furnished places rented by the day, week, or month, which are so necessary to a city with a large percentage of transients in its population. People are always coming to Washington or leaving it. It seems most of us are only passing through, no matter how long we've been here. Like me. I didn't start here, and I don't figure to end here, unless I wind up in an alley some night with the bright red flow of life running out of me.

She let me into the apartment. She stood facing me. She wore a simple charcoal dress, wool with three-quarter sleeves. "I haven't much time," she informed me.

"How did you meet Ted Fromann?" I asked her, explaining his background and use of an alias.

She wanted to call him Murray Atwood. She had known him only as Atwood. Her stuttering attempts to avoid using "Fromann" irritated me.

"Call him Peter Pan if it's easier for you," I told her.

We stood just inside the door to the apartment. She hadn't invited me to sit down. Now she did, as though to soften my irritability. We moved further into the living room.

I had seen apartments like that before. They all looked alike, and they all contained the same things: the tough-veneered furniture with the cigarette burns, the hard sofa-bed couches, the bare look, the empty feeling, the ache of homesickness. The people who occupied such apartments had left the comfort and ease of familiar surroundings in search of something new, either because they wanted to or because they had to. They were people on the go. And some of the ones I met were on the run.

Paula Devlin sat on the couch and lit a cigarette, while I asked the question again.

"I'm not sure," she said, exhaling smoke. "Is it important?"

"It could be," I assured her.

"At the theater," she said. "During intermission. He introduced himself to me in the Grand Foyer."

That would be the Kennedy Center. I could picture the scene. A crowd of people, milling about. A well-dressed human tide, some heading for the restrooms, others aimed toward the bar. A random meeting in those circumstances? I doubted it.

"Tell me, Mrs. Devlin, did you have a sense that Fromann had sought you out?"

She drew on her cigarette and expelled the smoke before answering, giving my question sober thought. "I hadn't thought about it," she said. "Why do you ask?"

I gave her the same analysis I had shared with Taffy, that of the odds against two people from different worlds meeting by chance. "Someone may have pointed Fromann in your direction," I said. "I'd like to know who that person was."

She shrugged, unconcerned. "It seemed at the time to be sheer coincidence," she said. "It remains that, for me. My unlucky night."

I pulled a straight-backed chair to a position in front of the couch and sat down. "Nobody seems to know anything about Fromann or the letters," I went on. "Ramirez didn't know and didn't believe me when I told him. Taffy didn't know, either."

"How can you be so sure?" she asked, palpably eager to get Taffy out of her hair by having him take the fall for Fromann's murder.

"When I told him about it a little while ago, he was too happy to hear it."

She stared at me. "You told him?"

"Relax. What's he going to do with the news? First, Devlin won't believe him. Second, how is Taffy going to explain how he knew? You wouldn't tell. If he says he heard it from Fromann it makes him a murder suspect. And if he tells Devlin that I told him, he's going to look like a fool or worse. Devlin's convinced I'm working something against him. He'll be suspicious of anything that comes from me."

She seemed to accept that analysis. At least she didn't argue with it. She just sat, smoking her cigarette, her eyes telling me nothing.

"So that brings me," I said, "to your husband. He's last on my list. If he didn't know about Fromann and the letters, who did?"

She snuffed out her cigarette in a green glass ashtray, not the sort you'd find in her Georgetown townhouse. "Suppose no one did," she said, without looking up at me. "Is it too difficult to conceive of someone killing him for reasons having nothing whatever to do with me or the letters?"

I could conceive of it, all right, but I didn't like it. "It's time for you to go to the police, Mrs. Devlin."

She laughed, a sound without any mirth to it. "Get out, Cronyn."

"No," I told her. "You overlooked something, Mrs. Devlin. You can't just deny ever seeing me or paying me to go to Fromann's apartment."

Her eyes questioned me.

"The money," I explained. "You had to get the ten thousand dollars someplace. If you took the money out of an account, it will show up in the record of your account activity. If you took it from a safe-deposit box, there will exist a record of you visiting your box. You can't walk away from that."

"I see," was all she said. She looked carefully at her

cigarettes, selected one, lit it, and stood up slowly. She walked to the window and looked out. She adjusted the Venetian blinds.

"Do you need help in rearranging the furniture?" I asked.

She turned back toward me. "I'm thinking about how much I should tell you," she replied.

"Why not all of it?"

She walked back to the couch and sat down. "Because it involves my husband." She took a deep drag on her cigarette and let it out through flared nostrils. "My problem is this, Cronyn. I want you out of my life, but if you go on thinking that you can connect me with the money you will think you have a handle on me."

"And I don't?"

"That's right. You only think you do, but as long as you do think it, you will feel free to bother me." Her eyes appraised me. "Against that, I have to balance the possibility of your using what I could tell you in a way that would be contrary to my husband's interests."

"Only if he killed Ted Fromann."

"Where I got that money has nothing to do with Fromann. And no record exists of where I obtained it."

"That's difficult to believe."

"You see what I mean," she said. "Unless I tell you, you will go on believing that you can establish my connection to the money." She paused and consulted the hot end of her cigarette, briefly, before meeting my eyes again. "I took it from the safe in my husband's study," she said.

"I once had a client who insisted that he could not have been guilty of a rape committed by a bareheaded man because the client always wore a hat. When asked to produce the hat, he couldn't do it, he said, because an elephant had stepped on it."

"You don't believe me."

142

"Let me say that I believe in practicalities, and so I ask myself if it is practical for a man to keep ten one-thousand-dollar bills in his home safe. I answer myself no, unless he hates to tell the newspaper boy to come back on payday."

She didn't seem impressed by my sarcasm. "He often keeps much more than that in the safe." She said it with a tone of direct simplicity. Some of my skepticism eroded.

"How much more?"

"A week ago I counted nearly two hundred fifty thousand."

A quarter of a million cash? It was my turn to stand up and walk around the room. The sum boggled the mind. Brother Devlin had his fingers into something the Internal Revenue Service probably didn't know about. If Paula Devlin told the truth, that is.

"It comes and goes," she added.

I walked back to the coffee table and looked down at her. "Like the sun?"

"I'm telling you where I got the money," she said. "If you want to look at my personal checking account, you can do so. I don't have a safe-deposit box."

I sat back down on the chair. Despite my natural caution, belief in what she said began to overtake doubt. "How much was in the safe on Monday?"

"Eighteen thousand," she answered promptly.

That answered the question of why she'd been in such a hurry to return home on Monday afternoon. It was her husband's money that I'd taken to Ted Fromann's place and she wanted to put it back where it belonged before Devlin noticed it was missing. It would have been interesting to see her get out of that pickle if she could not have put the money back, but I didn't go into that. I had another question.

"Did Fromann know about all that cash?"

"No."

"No? Isn't that the sort of thing a mistress might let slip to her lover in a moment of intimacy?"

"I never told him anything about the money."

I believed her, and the reason I believed her was the simplest in the world. If he had known about all that money, he'd have never settled for ten thousand.

"Where does this money come from?" I asked.

She shook her head. "I don't know."

"Where does it go, then?"

"I don't know." Voice strong, defiant. "The money is there. That's all I know about it."

"I'll bet your husband doesn't know that you know." She didn't answer. I went on. "If he knew you had lifted his safe combination, it might annoy him." The hard way to get into a safe is with dynamite or a blow torch. The easy way is to have the combination. You'll eventually give the combination away if you neglect the fundamentals, which are: you do not write down the combination. It's always the wrong person who will find it. You never use as a combination the first five or six digits of your telephone or social-security number or some obvious series of numbers like your date of birth. If I wanted to get into your safe, I'd make sure I knew those numbers too.

Finally, over time, a friend or relative or colleague who is particularly anxious to get into your safe is going to pick up a number here and a number there. The only way to prevent this from happening is to change the combination to your safe regularly. If you don't know how, get the company rep to show you and practice while he's there. With the door open, of course.

I stood up and went to the door. "I think you know where that money comes from, Mrs. Devlin. That knowledge could prove dangerous, should your husband find out, especially if he had reason to believe you could not be trusted. In that case, you'd need a place to run to, after cleaning out the safe." I looked around the room. "Someplace like this would do fine," I added. "Temporarily, at least."

I stopped at the desk on my way out of the building. The balding guy sitting there looked me over and didn't find anything to like. "Yes?" he said.

"My friend in 406," I said, "didn't say anything about a husband, but that's the sort of thing I like to be sure of. Fun's fun, but it's a long way down from the fourth floor."

He mellowed a bit when he saw the twenty in my hand. "I'll check the card," he said. He turned away to a file cabinet behind him. His body shielded what he did. He came back to me in two minutes.

"Major Rodgers is expected to join his wife within several days," he told me. "The Major is coming back from an overseas tour." His face held a blank look. He didn't care. He'd seen it all before. "She's cutting it pretty thin, if you ask me."

Well, if she wanted to keep her whereabouts a secret from Devlin, she would not use her own name. And without some kind of identification, the management might worry about renting her a place. They had to keep their eyes open for single ladies who wanted to go into business. The fictitious Army husband apparently had done the trick.

Despite her denial about needing a last resort, she was a careful lady, and if Walter Devlin believed his boy Taffy and pitched her out, she would not go empty-handed.

13

I WAITED UNTIL past five-thirty before calling Mary Thresher. She'd told me that she seldom arrived home from work before then, and I didn't want to talk to Dilly.

"A report to the client," I explained when she came on the phone. "I also wanted to know how it's going there."

"It's difficult to discuss over the telephone," she replied, her voice guarded. "Perhaps I should come to the store and see for myself."

"I'm at home," I said and gave her the address of the building on New Hampshire Avenue where I lived.

"As soon as I can," she said and hung up.

I had time to shower and shave and to put on faded jeans, a sweater, and soft, old loafers, before the guy at the desk in the lobby called to say that my guest had arrived. I waited for her at the door.

I took her coat. Underneath she wore a brown corduroy blazer, plain white blouse with mandarin collar, cherry slacks. She smelled nice. I hung her coat in the hall closet and came back looking for a drink order. She said whatever, and whatever became a small pitcher of Gibsons, which I put on the breakfast counter. We occupied the stools, knees almost touching.

She sipped and explained her reticence on the phone. "I told Dilly that you had to go out of town. She hasn't forgotten her idea to go to the police." Mary looked tired. "Rick, who lives downstairs from us, and his wife are coming to see her this evening. Have you found anything?"

I shook my head. "Not much," I told her. "I can't connect the most likely people with Fromann at all. It had to be someone who knew him, and I can't find anyone who did, other than the people out of his past, your sister and three others, all of whom have iron-clad alibis." I paused. "Except Dilly."

A long silence enveloped us. Then, "What do I do, Dan? Let her go to the police?"

I drank from my glass and thought of Paddock. I could almost see the wolfish look on his face when we brought Dilly to him. She wouldn't have a chance, and not the least because she was connected to me, my client, maybe my friend. His lips would flatten over his teeth, ready to go for the jugular.

"No," I said. "Not yet." I stood up and went to the freezer and brought more ice and replenished our glasses. "I haven't eaten."

It turned out that she hadn't either so I took two steaks from the freezer and thawed them in the microwave and started the coffeemaker. She offered to fix the salad, and I gave her free rein with what she could find. The freezer also provided us with a bag of frozen french fries, which I arranged on a pizza pan and put in the oven.

We ate at the counter. "Talk to me," I said.

"What about?"

"Anything," I suggested. "Everything."

"Will it help Dilly?"

"It might. You might know something that doesn't seem important. You might say something that gives me an idea. The nice thing about starting with nothing is that anything looks like something."

She looked dubious, but she started, haltingly. There were two brothers, one older than Dilly. That brother, I gathered, had the idea that being the oldest of the four siblings gave him the responsibility of telling the others what to do. Between Dilly and Mary came another brother who, together with a more than willing wife, was trying to repopulate the state of Ohio. She talked about herself—growing up, good grades in school, clubs, sports, cheerleading. She'd done two years at a junior college learning something about clothing design. It hadn't done her any good at the time since she was mainly interested in getting that social seal of approval that says a girl is a woman. A husband.

"I was twenty-one," she said. "He was twenty-three. It was supposed to last forever. I must have been sure that it would. I can't remember now. I had to have felt something, but it's all gone." She shook her head and looked down at her plate. There wasn't anything wrong with her appetite. Mine either. Even a hungry dog wouldn't have found much left.

"Coffee?"

She nodded, so I brought coffee to the living room, and we sat there, she on the couch. I pulled a chair from the dining room.

"All I can remember," she continued, "was the sense of failing, the sense of inadequacy." She looked beyond me, her eyes focusing into her own past. "Little things, you know. Like, I'd try to look good for him. Sometimes I'd feel pretty, but there'd always be something wrong, something that looked stupid. Maybe the wrong shoes or scarf or something. It's not that I didn't try." She paused. "Ever been married?"

"No. Well, maybe partially."

"Partially?" A question came to her eyes. She laughed, a good laugh that said she had stopped worrying over the past. It was just there, like the little scar on her cheek that you could hardly see unless you looked closely. "Let's do the dishes," she said.

We did, that is, we rinsed them and put them in the dishwasher.

"We had no children," she said, ending that period in

149

her life. "He found someone else. He got the divorce. I didn't care one way or the other."

We went back to the living room. "Is that when you came to Washington?"

"Soon afterwards. We got a call from Dilly one night. She was practically in hysterics. She'd been fired from her job. Somebody had to come and be with her. I wanted out of Ohio. Anywhere would have done. I flew into National that same night."

"What happened?"

She shrugged. "She had been working at one of the big department stores downtown, Woodies, in the credit department. On her way back from lunch one day, she thought she saw someone in the store she knew. By the time she reached the counter, the customer was gone," Mary took a deep breath. "Apparently she created quite a scene, right there on the main floor of the store. They had to let her go."

"She couldn't get her job back?"

"No. I talked to her employers. They were sympathetic, but they had already put up with quite a bit from her. They said that she had periods where she just drifted off to another world in the middle of her work. The scene on the main floor was the last straw." She paused. "I think they hated to do it, fire her, I mean. But they just couldn't have her going off like that over nothing and possibly embarrassing a valued customer. They put her on extended sick leave and, when that ran out, terminated her. You couldn't blame them."

"How did she explain it?"

"She didn't." Mary took a deep breath and expelled it. "I didn't handle it too well. I didn't know then how bad she was. It seemed to me that the scene was just a tantrum she had thrown over not getting her way. I told her to shape up or people would think she was crazy or something." She leaned forward and put her empty cup

150

on the coffee table. "I came down on her too hard. She withdrew into herself and refused to talk about it. If I mention it even now, she gets very angry."

"More coffee?"

She shook her head. "What now?" she asked.

"I'm going to start pushing people who don't want to be pushed."

Her eyes narrowed. "You know something that you aren't telling me."

"Yes. It won't help you to know."

"But it could hurt?"

I didn't say anything.

"Dan, these people . . ." she began, ". . . are they dangerous?"

"You don't know anything," I told her, "about anything. Your sister is all you know. Your sister knew Fromann, but that was years ago. You don't even know me. You've never been to my office or here."

"Dan . . ."

I stood up and went to the coat closet. She went with me and stood close as I opened the door to the closet. I could almost feel her warmth. It radiated toward me, carrying with it the scent of woman.

I turned to her. Our eyes met, hers round and suddenly a little surprised. I closed on her and took her in my arms and bent to kiss her mouth gently. Her luminous eyes closed slowly, and we clung to each other.

I lifted my head and searched her face for the look that said yes. I touched the tiny scar on her cheek with the tip of my finger.

"I fell," she said. "When I was six." She made no move to leave my embrace.

Our mouths sought each other hungrily and, after a while, we went to the bedroom, and there in the darkness we discovered each other. And in the soft wonder of her, we joined eagerly.

"I want to stay," she said, later.

"No. It's too dangerous."

A siren howled from New Hampshire Avenue, eight stories down. The sound of pain, often of death.

She shivered against me. "What . . ."

I held her. "They go by often. George Washington University Hospital is only a few blocks from here. They have a busy emergency room." Including a president a few years ago. "I'll go down with you."

I could feel her nodding in the dark. I disengaged my arms, sliding them over her smooth nudity. She let me go, reluctantly. I left the bed and dressed and waited for her in the living room. Then we went down together.

Between six and seven, when she had arrived, is the best time to find a parking spot in that neighborhood and even then you have to be lucky. She had been, finding one almost directly opposite the entrance to my building.

"Dan, be careful," she said.

I told her I would and watched her drive away, her tail lights disappearing in the traffic heading for Dupont Circle.

I turned.

Taffy stood behind me, all 275 pounds of bone and hard muscle, between me and the entrance to my building.

"He wants to see you," he said.

Behind him, through the story-and-a-half-high plate-glass windows that fronted my building, I could see the two massive cut-glass chandeliers in the lobby and the Christmas tree and the desk clerk, ignoring anything beyond the lobby itself, warm, secure. Outside, it was cold. Outside there was Taffy. Our breathing created little vapor clouds in front of our mouths.

I had wanted Devlin to make a move. Now that he had, I didn't want to toss away the opportunity. "Where?"

"At his place," Taffy replied. "The house in George-town." He stood balanced on legs like small tree trunks.

His eyes never left mine. He wasn't sure about my reaction and wasn't taking any chances.

Devlin might have given him orders to bring me in, if I objected to coming. My guess was that he hadn't. Too messy. Devlin wanted to talk. The place in Georgetown was a good spot for that, a bad one for any rough stuff. Devlin didn't strike me as a bird who would foul his own nest.

"All right, precious," I said. "Let's roll."

The house we went to was typical Georgetown. It was old, with tiny rooms and brick steps leading up to a heavy front door from a lumpy brick sidewalk.

Devlin himself let us in and parked us in the small living room. He told us to wait while he disappeared into a narrow hall leading deeper into the house.

The room in which we waited was furnished entirely in antiques or copies of antiques. I'm never sure. I suspected, however, that Devlin knew. The wood was dark, the fabrics hard. None of the plush modernity of his office.

Wood floors showed around the edge of a carpet that had a flowery design woven into it. Even it seemed to be an antique. One thing I missed in the place was lamps. I'm used to living rooms with lamps on tables. The omission nagged at me until I realized that he'd decorated the room to capture the flavor of its original decor, and there would have been no lamps then. Light from a small brass chandelier illuminated the room.

I saw no sign of Paula Devlin.

Devlin returned with an unopened bottle of Dewar's and two glasses, no ice, no water. He poured some in each glass and handed one to me. Taffy, apparently, used neither alcohol nor tobacco.

Devlin took his glass to the settee, sat down and crossed his legs. He was wearing black slacks and a pearl gray, brocaded smoking jacket. A blue ascot covered his throat.

I waited until Taffy had settled into a chair in the corner, out of the way. Then I chose a straight-back chair facing Devlin. I tried the whiskey, found it good, and said to Devlin. "It's your party."

"You're annoying me," he said. "I want it stopped."

"When you tell me who killed Ted Fromann and why."

He considered me out of calculating eyes. "What do you really want, Cronyn?"

"I just told you."

"That's cover. Taffy has another idea."

"I can't wait to hear it. I'll bet it's an original."

I looked at Devlin as I spoke but I kept Taffy well within my peripheral range of vision. If he moved, I was ready to move too. Only I didn't think Devlin had that sort of thing in mind. Not in his own house. The antique furniture wouldn't stand a chance if Taffy and I got serious about our feelings for one another.

"Taffy thinks that you and the dead man, Fromann, were partners," Devlin explained, "and that you and he tried to force Mrs. Devlin into an alliance to work against me. It has the ring of truth."

"The biggest problem with it," I replied, "is the notion that Taffy thinks. In the place where most people have a brain, Taffy has a muscle. His problem is that he can't get to it to exercise it."

Taffy stood up and took a step in my direction. I also stood and turned to meet him. "You going to start it?" I asked him.

"Taffy!" spoke Devlin sharply to his heavy hitter. "Sit down. Please."

Taffy stood undecided for a moment. The indecision passed. He glared at me, nodded toward Devlin, and retreated the step he had taken toward me. He sat down and curved his mouth into a semi-pout. "It'll be fun

154

when it happens," he said, and settled back to see his story shake the fruit from the tree.

I also sat back down. "Taffy has a problem," I told Devlin. "He wants Mrs. Devlin out of the picture, but he can't appear to be working against her or that would make you mad."

"You're a liar," interjected Taffy from his chair in the corner.

"Hush, Taffy," said Devlin. "He's deliberately trying to annoy you." To me he said, "On the contrary, Cronyn, Taffy sees Mrs. Devlin as the aggrieved party in your scheme."

"Well," I admitted. "I have to hand it to him. He's not as stupid as he seems. It's a good try."

Devlin looked puzzled. "What is?"

"His story. If you want to tell somebody something that the somebody won't believe if he hears it from you, you have a third party tell it. In this case, I'm the third party. In order to save my ass, I'm supposed to tell you what the real connection between me and Fromann and Mrs. Devlin is."

"I'm waiting to hear it," said Devlin.

"No way," I told him. "If I tell everything I know, and you don't, then you hold all the cards. Bad deal for me."

"I already hold all the cards," Devlin said.

"If you did," I pointed out, "I wouldn't be here. You wouldn't be worried about me."

"He's lying, Mr. Devlin," said Taffy from his corner. "He doesn't know anything, except about Mrs. Devlin."

They had me in an awkward position. I could not watch both of them at the same time. I wanted to watch the reaction on Devlin's face to see when I had scored, but I also had to watch Taffy. I couldn't afford to let him have the first unchallenged move. It was all the edge he needed. I kept my eye on him.

"Speaking about lies," I said. "Explain the one where

you just happened to run into Mrs. Devlin outside my office building."

Taffy, smoothly, to Devlin, "I knew that he was up to something. I was watching his building."

"If your boy was worried about me, why didn't he tell you?"

Devlin's eyes narrowed. He was looking at Taffy. "Well?"

Taffy gulped. "It's all Paula's fault," he said. "She was seeing the dead guy on the side, Walter, I swear it."

Devlin looked disbelieving.

Taffy tried to overcome the disbelief. "She even wrote him dirty letters," he went on. "She hired Cronyn to get them back." He looked at me. "Tell him, you sonofabitch, tell him what you told me yesterday."

"Sure," I said, "that's what happened."

Taffy's face held a look that mixed surprise and relief.

"But," I said, "she'll deny it. She'll say that I made up the story and told Taffy about it. She and Taffy agree on one thing only, that I'm a notorious liar."

"I'd like to see those letters," said Devlin. "If they exist." He gave me a grim look. "Who has them now? You?"

"Not me, I replied. "Nobody. They're gone, burned."

"How convenient." He looked at Taffy. "I hope you aren't in this with him. I warned you about your juvenile jealousy."

Taffy paled. "No, Walter, honest to God. I never believed him. Never. He told me that story. I tried to protect you and Paula. You know that I'd never do anything against you. You know that."

"Ha," I said. "He'd been following her."

Devlin did not look happy with his pal. "You haven't anything better to do? With tens of thousands of dollars at stake and you can take time out to spy on my wife? She carries out her duties to my complete satisfaction,

Taffy. I'm not sure, under the circumstances, that I can say the same about you."

"He's lying, Mr. Devlin," said Taffy with a whine of desperation in his voice. "I did not follow Mrs. Devlin."

This was getting me nowhere, but I thought I saw Taffy's weak spot. He had admitted to me that he had followed Paula Devlin to the Northwest Gardens Apartments. He had not said when, but the last time she visited Fromann was the previous Saturday, and that sounded about right for Taffy to have followed her. If he had followed her on an earlier visit, he would not have waited until Wednesday to have come to see me. I was sure I was on solid ground, so I made a suggestion to Devlin.

"Why not ask him what he was doing last Saturday?" I said. "Either he admits to having followed her, or he'll have to leave a big gap to be filled in." It sounded good to me, but I had not included everything in my calculations. I had left out that I might be wrong.

Devlin stared at me for a long second. "Taffy and I were together all day Saturday," he said.

That wasn't what I expected to hear. And I couldn't reconcile it with all that I had been told. I could see no reason for Devlin to lie for Taffy. There had to be another answer. All I needed was time to look for it. Only Devlin was not giving me time for anything.

His eyes turned cold. "You're finished, Cronyn. Close your office and leave Washington. Maybe you thought you could shake me down or cut yourself in, but it didn't work. You gambled and you lost."

He stood up and went to a phone discreetly concealed in an antique cabinet. He dialed a lot of numbers. Long distance.

"No names," he said into the telephone. "Do you know who this is?" He paused. A small smile came to his face. "It's nice to be remembered," he continued. "I have a problem. I must speak to Helga." Pause. "I'll be right here." He hung up.

He took a cigarette from his silver case, fitted it to his silver holder and lit it. "You are playing for keeps, Cronyn." he said.

I was his problem, the one he needed to talk to Helga about. I decided that it would be a good idea to stick around and hear the rest of the conversation.

I helped myself to more whiskey. Taffy sat immobile in the corner, his feet flat on the floor, his hands on his knees. Somewhere further back in the house, a clock played us a tune of Westminster chimes and struck eleven times.

The phone rang.

"Yes," said Devlin, into it. He listened. He replied, reading from my card, giving my name and address, both office and home. "He's a private investigator." A brief question from the other end. "Yes, a complete removal. Nothing in between if he continues to be a problem." A long period of silence. "I understand. Agreed." He fished a pen from his shirt pocket and wrote something on a pad. "I'll call this number, if necessary. Yes. Thank you." He hung up.

"What good is he," I asked Devlin, motioning toward Taffy, "if you have to contract out the heavy stuff?"

"Let me," said Taffy. It sounded like a plea.

Devlin shook his head. He spoke to me. "You know him, Cronyn, and you'd be looking for him. I don't know how good you are, and I don't like to take chances. This way you'll never know who it's going to be until it's too late."

He was right. It would be a lot more effective his way. The hitman could be my next client. He could be a panhandler on the street, a bum on a steam grating, a substitute janitor in my apartment building. He could be anybody or everybody, and you can't watch out for everybody.

158

"How much am I worth, Devlin?"

"Ten thousand. They assume that you carry a gun. That makes the risk a little higher."

"That's a lot of money."

"There's a lot at stake."

I didn't doubt him. Paula Devlin had seen as much as a quarter of a million in Devlin's safe. Still, he didn't strike me as someone who'd spend ten thousand bucks unless he had to.

"Suppose I take you up on your offer to leave town?"

He smiled. "That's sensible. If you take that option, you may very well live a long and happy life."

"The point in bringing me here," I suggested, "was so I could hear you make that telephone call. To scare me."

"A threat isn't much good unless it's backed up, Cronyn. That was the purpose of the phone call, so that you'd know I had both the intention and the means to remove you, permanently, from my affairs."

"Okay," I said. "I'll steer clear of you from now on."

"Not good enough. I mean to be sure of you. You'll either go far away, or you will die."

The sound of rain beating against my bedroom window woke me. In the half-light that is the city at night, I saw a tall shadow standing in the doorway.

Fear melted my insides.

For what seemed an eternity I lay there, breathing rapidly, heart pounding. Motionless with terror. Helpless before the enemy who comes in the dark.

Then the moment passed. It was, after all, only a shadow, my robe hung carelessly over the corner of the half-open door. I turned on the bedside light, got up and took down the robe, hung it in my closet and went back to bed. I reached for the light, turned it off and laid my hand carefully down beside me.

It was shaking.

14

THE RAIN TURNED to a wet snow before stopping at daybreak, making the sidewalks temporarily white and glistening and the streets hazardous for the Thursday morning commuters.

I packed a beat-up canvas bag that I'd bought from an Army-surplus store and drove the station wagon to a motel in Silver Spring called the Twenty Grand. The people who run the place know me. I wanted the end room away from the street, and I got it.

I didn't think Devlin was all that anxious to spend his ten thousand getting rid of me until he saw whether or not he could scare me off. That gave me some time to work on getting him off my case. In case I was wrong, I wanted him to have to work at finding me, which meant I needed another place to sleep.

I called Mary Thresher and told her not to try to call me. After that the subway took me to Dupont Circle, and a cab took me to the curb in front of the embassy where Ramirez worked. I got out, crossed the sidewalk and went between yellow-stone portals into a small courtyard just large enough to turn a limousine around. This was the business end of the place. I mounted two low, stone steps, pushed open one side of a heavy glass-and-bronze door and found myself in a large marble-floored room with a two-story ceiling and brass sconces containing electric candles on the walls.

I told the heavy-chested woman at the reception desk that I had come to see Mr. Ramirez-Pondal and after we had a round or two about not having an appointment and her making a call to somebody, she let me go up the stairs to Ramirez's office.

The office looked more like somebody's living room than it did an office. It contained a couch, end tables, coffee table, two easy chairs, and a semi-large writing table and chair in front of two tall, narrow windows that looked like French doors. The carpet was a neutral gray and the rest of the fabrics were predominantly burgundy.

A flag stood in one corner. Portrait reproductions of two nineteenth-century gents flanked the windows. On another wall was a large color photo of a cherubic-looking man with cruel eyes dressed in a military uniform that featured a chest full of ribbons and medals. Since I was pretty sure Ramirez's country had not fought a war in this century, I figured the ribbons and medals were only there to distinguish the president from the doorman at the presidential palace.

Ramirez met me at his door with a handshake and a grin that said he was glad to see me. He gave every appearance of meaning it.

He sat me down in one of the easy chairs and put himself in the other one. I declined his offer of a drink.

"I meant to call you," he said. "I have two tickets to the 'Skins game Sunday. Can you make it? Last game of the season, you know."

"I'm working, Carlos."

He kept on grinning for a second or so after I spoke. Then the grin gradually faded as the meaning of the words began to sink in. He put on his diplomatic smile, good enough I supposed, if you hadn't seen the sincerity of his welcoming grin moments before.

"Ah, well then," he said. "Fire away. An indiscreet wife? An outraged husband? I plead my innocence."

"Didn't Devlin tell you about our little chat last night?

162

About how you didn't have to worry about me anymore?"

The last remnant of a smile faded. "Sorry," he said.
"What was that again?"

"I'll spell it out for you."

"That would be best."

"Devlin's a crook. He's always been a crook, but he
broke off from his old pals and found himself a nifty little
influence-peddling operation. One of the things that
makes it so nifty is that he does things for people in the
government who do things for him. If one of his contacts
likes a toot now and then, Devlin can line up a contact.
Of course, nobody knows that Walter is behind the
contact, so he makes out two ways: gratitude for the
contact and profit on the sale of the cocaine."

Ramirez fiddled with the knot of his tie. "Who told you
all this?" he asked.

"Some is conjecture, but it's based on picking up a
little here and a little there."

"What does that have to do with me?"

"I want you to confirm it. The only way I can get
Devlin off my back is to put him in jail. You could go to
the cops, Carlos, and back me up on this."

He shook his head. "I'm sorry, Cronyn," he replied.
"I like you, but I don't know what you're talking about.
If you and Walter are having a tiff, I'm sure that you can
patch it up."

"Walter wants me dead. I sat in his house last night
while he put out a contract on me with his old pals in
Miami."

Carlos stopped fiddling with his tie. He held his hand
suspended in midair while he stared at me. He tried a
smile that had no life behind it.

I went on. "There's a woman named Jacquie Germaine. She's running coke out of a massage parlor.

Makes a good front, I guess. Cops take it for granted that she's operating a movable whorehouse. There aren't enough cops in the Western Hemisphere to keep track of all the people who pay for sex in this town. So the cops leave her alone."

"It sounds like a long way from Walter Devlin," Ramirez observed casually. "Or from me."

"You bring the stuff in, Carlos," I said. "That's the reason for these little trips back home every month or so. It's easy for you to get it through customs. You just walk it through, covered by your diplomatic immunity. When you leave Dulles Airport, you head straight for Jacquie's massage parlor."

He started to deny it. I didn't let him.

"Remember Pappy MacClearn? He earned that thousand from you the other night, didn't he? Or was it more?"

"Yeah," he replied. "Yeah. I remember."

"The next step, probably, is for Jacquie to repackage the stuff into retail-size quantities, ounces would be favored. I'd think. Her girls deliver it. If I tried to say how the contact is made between Jacquie and the customer, I'd only be guessing, so I'll skip that."

Carlos stood up and went to the French doors and looked out.

I spoke to his back. "As the cocaine is sold, Jacquie sends the proceeds to Devlin, after taking her cut," I said. "The cash builds up in his safe at the Georgetown house, up to as much as a quarter of a million bucks. Then, poof, it's gone again, usually about the same time you make one of your casual visits to Devlin."

He turned away from the window. "Conjecture?"

"No. Fact."

He shook his head. "Only Walter could know that. He wouldn't tell you." He paused, thinking. Slowly a new awareness overtook him. It showed in his face. "Paula," he said. His guess needed no confirmation from me.

"He gives you the money," I went on. "Some for you, some to buy more cocaine, and probably some for deposit to his account in a South American branch of a Swiss bank. The circle closes."

He returned to his writing table and sat down. He couldn't look at me. "I shall, of course, deny all of this," he said.

"It's over, Carlos. Finished. And you can't be touched because of your diplomatic immunity. You can go to the police and sing the whole song and all they can do is send you home."

He arranged a few papers on his desk. He lifted his eyes and let his glance wander around the room. He set his jaw and looked at me.

"I like all this, Cronyn," he said. "At first I thought it was a laugh. Me as a striped-pants cookie pusher? Get outta here, I thought, but what the hell? It got me back to the States, living in comfort, lots of parties, forty miles away from a big-league ballpark, no work. A gas."

He lifted the edge of the blotter on the table and took two oblong pieces of cardboard from under it. He looked at them. "A gas," he repeated.

He looked back at me. "That's what I thought. You know what changed it? Arranging a little loan for a damned little cement-block building where people who never saw money can make buttons—buttons for godsakes—and earn a wage and build a new clinic and a new school." He took a deep breath and expelled it. He looked up at the ceiling.

Neither of us said anything. He'd given me his answer. His coke-smuggling days were over. We both knew it, but he'd be no help to me in saving my life. Even if I went to the cops with what I knew about his role in the drug ring, it wouldn't help. He could just pull the cloak of diplomatic immunity around him. The cops couldn't even talk to him unless he wanted to talk, and he didn't.

I stood up. "I wouldn't give much for Paula Devlin's chances if you tell Devlin about this conversation," I said.

He nodded. I turned and headed for the door.

"Cronyn." He came around his desk and caught up to me. He had the two tickets to the last Redskins' game in his hand. He handed them to me. "Take somebody you like well enough to share a bottle with, for keeping-warm purposes."

I looked at the pair of tickets. "I don't figure I'd enjoy it much, Carlos."

I turned and walked out of Ramirez's office, feeling like I had just blindsided Mister Rogers.

The man walking toward me down the center aisle of the church had a round, open face done in chocolate brown. He also wore a white clerical collar and a dark blue suit.

"How can I help you, officer?" he asked, making an assumption which said more for the neighborhood than it did for him or me. I don't think I looked like a plain-clothes cop, and I didn't figure he had anything to feel guilty about. It's just that I had probably the only white skin within a mile, so nine guesses out of ten, that made me The Law.

"Not a cop," I told him. "I was told that I could find Jacquie Germaine here." That wasn't quite a lie. When I had called the massage service number, a recording wanted me to leave a message. So I called around to a few people looking for someone who knew Jacquie and who knew that she had gotten religion and where she went to church every day.

"Sister Germaine is at prayer," the man in front of me said.

I looked beyond him. She sat about three rows back from the front of the church, her back to me. Two other women sat alone in the church but Jacquie was unmistakable. Her fat shoulders sloped like a pyramid down to the spreading hips hidden by the curving back of the wood pews. She wore what looked like a white silk handkerchief over her head as she bowed to her devotions.

"You're the Reverend Farnsworthy?" I asked. The sign outside, announcing the topic of the next sermon, gave the name of the Reverend E. Washington Farnsworthy.

"Yes, brother. Welcome to the Eternal Glory of God Temple."

"Mind if I wait?"

"Compose your soul, brother. This is the Dwelling of Jesus Christ, your Savior, a House of Peace and Calm. This is not the place for the worldly concerns which agonize your spirit." He turned and glanced toward the heavy bulk that was the object of my attention. "Wait in the vestibule. I'll tell her you want to see her."

"The name is Dan Cronyn. She knows me."

He looked me over. "Sister Germaine brings great joy and comfort to this assembly of sinners seeking Christ. If she doesn't want to see you, that is her right. You understand?"

I nodded and retreated to the tiny vestibule. The doors swung closed behind me. The vestibule was cooler than the place where Jacquie Germaine, whorehouse madam and dope dealer, prayed.

Hypocritical? Maybe, but I figured she must have needed what the Reverend Farnsworthy had to offer. In return, I supposed that the joy and comfort she brought to the congregation arrived in the form of cash.

The doors opened and she rolled through, a jiggling blob of flesh. She carried a large canvas bag over her left shoulder. What looked like a leather-bound bible showed its corner out of the top of the bag. "Outside," she said, and pushed through the front doors.

The little church, probably once the property of a long-departed mainline denomination, stood above the quiet tree-lined street. A wide sidewalk connected the church steps to a half-dozen concrete steps leading to the city sidewalk. They were wide steps with an iron pipe railing going up the middle.

I followed her down those steps to the sidewalk. She turned. "Whatta ya want, Cronyn?"

"Did your girl, Sissy, tell you about me?"

"Yeah. She told me."

"And you told Devlin."

Her eyes, seeming lost in deep pockets of flesh, glittered. "Who?"

I heard a car door slam. I turned a little. The thin guy from the massage service office strolled along the sidewalk toward us, blowing on his hands, a cigarette dangling from his lips. Through the half-zipped front of his leather jacket I could see the white sweater. I loosened up and rode forward a little on my feet.

"Stop screwing around, Jacquie. You're working for Devlin."

"Problem, Jacquie?" said White Sweater, coming up to us.

"I can handle it," she told him. "Get the car warmed up." He strolled away. She looked at me. "Don't know the man."

"Sure, Jacquie. Just like you don't know Carlos Ramirez. Sissy didn't tell you everything, did she?"

"The little shit told you that she knew Ramirez?"

"That's right. I had her in a bind. She was on a

delivery. She didn't tell me that. I saw the stuff for myself. When I mentioned cops, she'd have told me anything. She was scared, Jacquie, scared that she'd be caught holding. She didn't want to take the rap for you, just like I don't think you want to take the rap for Devlin."

She said nothing. Her eyes did the talking for her. They were saying, go on, turkey, dig your hole a little deeper.

"I've just come from Carlos. I know the whole deal, Jacquie. I tip the narcs, and they raid your place on 14th Street. You're caught holding. Why do the time for Devlin, Jacquie?"

Her fleshy jowls moved. "Where do you come in, Cronyn?"

"I know too much for Devlin to sleep well. He offered me a choice—either I leave town permanently or he puts a contract out on me."

"So leave town."

"I like it here. If I go someplace else I have to start all over. What are my chances of that, do you suppose, when the word gets around that I was handed my hat and run out of D.C.? Besides, suppose Walter thinks later that he'd be a whole lot more comfortable if he never had to worry about me coming back, ever."

"Sounds like you have a real problem," she said and turned away. "Stay away from my girls," she added, as an afterthought.

"You'll have to shut down the whole operation," I told her back. "Either that or risk getting caught holding the coke. What about a deal?"

She stopped and rotated her bulk back to me. "What deal?"

"I heard that Jacquie Germaine never went into anything without knowing first where the back door was," I said. "If you get caught holding, you have no out. You can't make much of a deal with the prosecution when you're caught cold. Plea bargain, maybe. That's all."

"What are you saying, Cronyn?"

"You and I go to the cops. I tell them everything. You just sit there. They haven't any real evidence against you. If they want to break up the operation and nail the head boy, Devlin, they need you. You hold out for immunity."

"Sure," she said. "Listen, Cronyn. What the hell do I care what your problem with Devlin is? If I have to shut down for a while, why do I need the cops? So I shut down. Big deal."

"Devlin won't like it. He has too much riding on keeping his customers happy."

"He's got no choice," she said. "He's smart enough to know that I have the other option, the one that you just mentioned."

By coming to Jacquie to get her help, I had warned her. She could close the operation now and leave me with nothing, not even the possibility of having one of her girls caught holding the coke. At least that way the cops would have believed my story about a drug ring. They might have even visited the prominent Mr. Devlin and asked him about it, and he could have told the story of my trying to pull something on him and his socially acceptable wife, extortion probably. In the meantime, something very nasty would happen to me, and the cops would call it a "drug-related gang killing."

I had no choice in any event. To bring Devlin down before he brought me down, I had to have someone on the inside. As I went for each of them in their turn, the whole picture began melting away before my eyes.

"You can't trust him, Jacquie," I told her, more in desperation than in the hope that it would change her mind.

170

She gave me one more look from her glittering eyes as she began to rotate her bulk once again toward the car. "Fuck off," she said.

I wanted to detain her by a mild tug on her arm. Instead, I grabbed the canvas bag she carried. Then I saw a silver-plated twenty-five automatic appear in her right hand. Jacquie moved a lot faster than you'd think.

So did White Sweater. I didn't hear the car door slam this time because he didn't bother. He appeared next to me, knife against my ribs, breathing heavily. Cigarettes will do that to you.

"Don't make another move," he said.

Jacquie Germaine backed away toward the car. When she got there, she put the gun back inside her coat and squeezed herself into the back seat and slammed the door and rolled down the back window and called for White Sweater. She too was breathing hard and her brow glistened with beads of perspiration.

"Where's your shooter?" he went on.

"I don't carry," I told him.

His eyes looked suspicious. "You lying, man, and you dead."

My mouth felt very dry, and sweat trickled down my ribs from my armpits. "I don't carry," I repeated.

I could feel the point of the knife through my clothes. It made concentrating on anything else difficult. Something other than perspiration rolled down my side. Blood. He had pricked my skin.

He was scared. We were both scared. Only he was the one with the knife. That made all the difference.

Jacquie called to him again from the car. "Put it away," she ordered. "Let's get the hell away from here."

I felt the knife disengage from my ribs, leaving only a slight burning sensation as salty perspiration seeped into the tiny cut it had left.

The skinny black guy retreated toward the car, his

hand on his rear pocket. No knife was visible. He got into the car behind the wheel, put it into gear and spun away from the curb.

The last I saw of Jacquie's face was of her staring back at me from the half-opened window of the rear door, her eyes nearly lost in flabs of flesh, one loose cheek flattened against the glass.

I drove back to the Twenty Grand Motel. My room looked untouched, just as it should have looked. The large canvas suitcase still stood at the foot of the bed. It held nearly a week's clothing, which had not yet found its way into the drawers of the built-in dresser.

I emptied the contents of the suitcase into the dresser and lay on the bed, thinking that the Twenty Grand may as well have been in Butte, Montana, as in Silver Spring, Maryland. Before the day was over, Jacquie would have closed down the operation and stashed the coke someplace. Maybe she'd tell Devlin about it first; maybe not. He might hear of her action first from a disappointed customer needing a snort or two. Whichever way he heard, Walter Devlin would likely be upset, but just how upset was a matter I could only guess at. Jacquie had better know what she was doing.

I left the bed, went to the window and looked out at the parking lot, empty but for my station wagon. There was nothing now to take to the cops. If Jacquie had been caught with the stuff, she'd have taken Devlin down with her in order to make the best deal she could make. Now, nothing. I had no handle over Jacquie if she stashed or dumped the cocaine.

On the other hand there was Devlin to consider. It was his coke, not Jacquie's. He might consider that Jacquie was expendable, but I doubted he would give up his merchandise so easily.

The empty canvas suitcase caught my attention and set my mind off on a new track. I tried to estimate how much coke Ramirez could have brought in on Monday. Not a lot. One suitcaseful, probably. Devlin wasn't running a big operation. He had a small group of selected clients, people who wouldn't or couldn't know where to go for their coke. And Devlin kept himself out of it.

If Assistant Secretary or Deputy Commissioner Caspar Q. Bureaucrat seemed interested in buying some reliable stuff, Devlin would suggest that he might know someone who knew someone. Eventually Caspar would receive a call. From Taffy? Probably. The call would tell Caspar to be in such-and-such room at such-and-such motel at the appointed time, if Caspar was still interested. Caspar would not know Taffy, nor would he know the girl who delivered the cocaine, nor would he know that he was buying the stuff from Walter Devlin. All that Caspar knew was that he had a friend in Walter, a friend who could put him in contact with a terribly discreet source of coke.

Back to estimating Ramirez's load. A small, tight operation. And Ramirez hauled the stuff every month or so in his luggage. Twenty, maybe thirty pounds, I guessed. More than one suitcase would have been hard to handle and possibly risky, raising questions. How many clothes does a person need for a weekend anyway?

So not a lot of cocaine, but enough. Not the sort of thing Devlin would like to see flushed down the toilet. Definitely not.

I turned away from the window and looked around the room. It would have to be headquarters for a while. And for that, I needed some things from the office. Sourcebook, Rolodex, Scotch. The canvas bag would do to haul the stuff I needed back to the room. I'd have to do it today. I couldn't count on being able to go back to the office tomorrow. Especially not after Jacquie told Devlin I was the reason she had to break off the operation.

I took the big canvas suitcase and went out to the car and drove under leaden skies back to the office, thinking that it could already be too late to consider Butte, after all.

15

PAULA DEVLIN CROSSED the lobby of my office building with a purposeful walk. She wanted to see me, she informed me, right then. Her face was grim.

We went up together in the elevator. She eyed my bag, but she said nothing about it.

I unlocked the door and let us in, me going first, carefully. The office was empty, quiet, undisturbed. I put the suitcase in the corner near the file cabinets and asked Mrs. Devlin what I could do for her.

Her eyes focused a steady glance on me. "When I returned home from the theater last night, Walter and Taffy were . . ." she hesitated slightly ". . . engaged. This morning, Walter had gone before I arose, which is not unusual. He often has breakfast with a client or a government contact before going to the office. What *was* unusual was that Taffy had spent the night in my house."

While she talked, I took off my raincoat and hung it on the coat tree and sat down in my chair. I suggested that she also make herself comfortable, but she declined. She didn't have the appearance of someone who wanted to be comfortable. She continued standing, going only as far as unbuttoning the front of her coat.

"Taffy suggested that I leave Walter," she said. "The way he said it sounded like an ultimatum."

"I'll bet. Taffy must be feeling his oats."

"He said you are finished, and that you can't help me."

"Did he say why I should want to?"

"Because we were partners in working against Walter," she replied.

"If your husband believes that," I said, "then you're in trouble, Mrs. Devlin. Did darling Taffy explain why?"

"He suggested I ask you."

"Your husband, Mrs. Devlin, plans to have me killed," I told her. "At the moment I'm okay because he's giving me one last chance to get out of town and, in addition, he doesn't want to spend the ten thousand bucks it'll cost him to have the job done right. Not, at least, until it's necessary."

She stared at me. At first her face was full of disbelief, which slowly ebbed and gave way to solemn concern. I doubted that her concern was for me. She sat down on the chair in front of my desk and shrugged herself out of her coat.

"Your husband is dealing cocaine, Mrs. Devlin," I went on. She affected a little gasp of surprise. "It's a nice little operation with no loose ends, except an unforeseen one." I leaned back in the chair, and the big spring sounded off. "Somebody killed Ted Fromann."

Her eyes narrowed. "He was part of a drug ring?"

"No. First of all, he wasn't living high enough off the hog for that. Second, there aren't any vacancies in your husband's operation. Third, Fromann comes from a different world than your husband. Devlin put together his little organization from people he knew and trusted. His acquaintance with his distributor came from his days of trying to organize small rackets in D.C. His importer probably was recommended to him by the Miami interests for whom he used to work. They'd have Latin American connections, probably."

She was shaking her head as I talked. "Walter? I can't believe that. He's a respected businessman. What are you trying . . ."

I cut her short. "Forget the innocent act," I told her.

176

"You knew about the cash in your husband's safe. You connected Ramirez with it. You noticed that whenever Ramirez came to chat about business, the money disappeared from the safe."

"Where did you get that . . ."

I didn't let her get any farther. "You also knew that those visits to your husband occurred as Carlos was on his way to the airport for one of his weekend trips to South America."

Her eyes, blank, watched me. She said nothing. She waited for me to arrive at the bottom line.

"Everybody," I went on, "knew that Carlos had a mistress back home. That was his cover for those frequent visits. Who could doubt such a story, especially when it involved a man with a reputation like his? That must have made you feel like what, Mrs. Devlin? Third in line, behind the long-suffering wife and the other mistress?" I waited for her to speak.

She didn't. She set her jaw. Her mouth became a line across her face.

"You would not have put up with that," I continued. "Sure, you had to accept the wife. That's a given when you become involved with a married man. But you didn't have to accept the other mistress. Carlos had no other mistress, did he, Mrs. Devlin? Either in South America or anywhere else."

She started a lie. "Everybody knows Carlos," she began. She paused. "No. There were no mistresses."

"There probably never had been," I suggested. "Before you, that is. He wanted you badly enough to tell you the real reason he was making those trips back home."

Her eyes gave nothing away as she looked at me. It was like peering into the face of the Sphinx.

"You knew that he was carrying cocaine." No reply. "He cared for you, Mrs. Devlin. Probably still does, a little."

177

She looked away. Whatever her thoughts were at that moment she was keeping them to herself.

"You told me," I went on, "that Carlos wasn't any type, when I tried to put him in the category of typical macho Latin lover." She made no comment. "You didn't have to defend him," I added.

She almost smiled. "Carlos is a most misunderstood man," she said. "He doesn't even understand himself. He allows himself to be defined by other people's perceptions of him. He . . . ," she broke off whatever it was she had been about to say. "It was a totally impossible situation."

"Yeah," I replied. "I can see why you'd think that. So you broke if off." I paused. "And rushed into Ted Fromann's arms. Bad trade, Mrs. Devlin."

"Women can be foolish."

"Not you, Mrs. Devlin. That's partly why you broke off your affair with Carlos. You wanted a bedmate, not someone whom you had begun to care about. Caring leaves one vulnerable, and you want never to be vulnerable."

She looked away toward one of my chalk drawings. "May I have a glass of water, please?"

I went to the cooler and brought us back each a cup of water.

The request for water was a signal that she wanted to change the subject. That was all right with me. Carlos Ramirez was the kind of a guy who could get under your skin, the kind of a guy with whom you wish things had turned out differently. Maybe she felt that way, too. I wasn't sure. She wasn't a woman you could ever be sure about.

"So what did Taffy want you to do?" I asked.

"To write a confession to Walter, admitting my affair and the letters and the blackmail." The grim look returned to her face.

178

"And the alternative?"

"To be considered your partner," she replied, "with all that entails." She stopped. Her finger nervously tapped on the top of her purse. "If I left him, would you tell him about the apartment in Virginia?

"No," I said. She looked at me with anxious eyes. I shrugged and added, "But then you can never be entirely sure, can you?"

"Damn you," she said. The look in her eyes told me that she didn't much like me.

"I have another idea," I said.

"A proposition?"

"Something like that."

She stood up. "Thanks," she said, a dryness in her voice. "But no thanks. A partnership with a dead man doesn't appeal to me."

"So you're ready to pack up and leave with what you can carry, two suitcases and the twenty or thirty thousand that has come into Walter's safe since Monday. You'll leave behind an eight-thousand-dollar wardrobe, the Georgetown address and the antiques, all of Walter's other legitimate investments, and a secret Swiss bank account."

"It's all Walter's," she said. "And he'd keep it in a divorce. I have to take what I can carry with me and disappear."

"I wasn't talking about divorce. If Walter and Taffy were in jail, you'd be left to take care of all Walter's possessions. You're a smart girl, Mrs. Devlin. Surely, given the time he's in the slammer, you could figure out a way to get more than what you could take from his safe now."

She looked at me with interest. She sat back down in the chair in front of my desk. "What do you have in mind?"

"Devlin doesn't know it yet but his distributor plans to

retire. When Devlin finds out, I think he's going to want the coke. I would imagine that there is enough of the stuff to fill at least a small suitcase, since it has been only four days since Carlos returned from his last run."

"How much is it worth?"

I shook my head. "I can't be sure. Twenty-five pounds of the purest stuff would likely have a street value of a half-million or more."

The numbers impressed her. "Go on," she said.

"Devlin probably gets less. His influence with the people who buy the stuff rests on the fact that he lines them up with a source who sells top-rated stuff cheaper than they can get it elsewhere."

"I understand."

"When he gets the cocaine back from his distributor, he's going to have to store it someplace, at least for a day or two. He's not likely to keep it in his office. There'd be too much chance that one of his employees would stumble on to it."

"He could keep it at home," she suggested. Her eyes gleamed. "Whoever owned the house during Prohibition had a hidden liquor cabinet installed. We don't use it, but it's still there."

"That's the place, then."

"What do you want me to do?"

"Call me here and leave a message as soon as he brings the cocaine home. I'll tip the cops. They'll do the rest."

She didn't like it. "No. That leaves me just sitting there waiting for you to show up here and get my message. Suppose he began to suspect something?"

She had a point. It was a risk for her, one she'd take because of the reward involved but also one she'd minimize if she could. That was one argument in favor of my giving her the motel number. The other argument had to do with the cops. I didn't know how soon they could put together a raid or how soon they could get a search warrant. Those sorts of things take time, and I couldn't be sure how long Devlin would keep the cocaine at home.

"All right," I agreed. "I'm at the Twenty Grand Motel in Silver Spring." I gave her the number on a piece of note paper. "I'll stay by the phone."

She looked at the paper. "As soon as I'm sure the cocaine is in the house," she said. "I'll call you. Then I'm leaving." She stood up to go.

I nodded. I expected it. "Don't make it too obvious. You might make him suspicious."

She put on her coat and started for the door.

"Mrs. Devlin," I said. "One more thing. Would your husband cover for Taffy? In a case of murder, I mean?"

"My husband would not cover for his own mother, unless he had a financial stake in the matter."

"That's what I thought. Yet he as much as covered for Taffy. Taffy had admitted to following you to Northwest Gardens, but when I mentioned it last night, your husband said that Taffy had been with him all day on Saturday of last week."

She peered at me. "What does it mean?"

"I don't know. It's like a dream in which you miss your bus and you run after it. You run and run, and the bus always seems just out of reach, and the only reason that you keep running is because of the belief you'll eventually catch the bus. Eventually, I'll catch the meaning of Devlin's coverup. Then I'll know what it means and whether it's important."

"Yes," she said, thoughtfully. "Yes, of course."

I stood at the window for a long time after Paula Devlin left my office. Outside, the rain slanted down in gray lines, darkening the street below, emptying it of all but the most determined passers-by.

Paula Devlin had given me an opening to her husband, but nothing I could do would make it move faster.

The telephone rang. I answered it.

Mary Thresher's voice, sounding as heavy as the skies outside my window, told me that what she had feared had happened.

Dilly had gone to the cops.

"While I was at work," Mary told me.

We sat at the kitchen table. Dilly slept in her bedroom. She had had a tiring day. Mary held my hand.

"The local police?" I asked.

Mary nodded. "Yes. Some of them know her." She paused. "She told them that she killed Fromann. They called me at work to come for her. They didn't believe her. As I said, they know her."

"They'd make allowances for that," I said. "If they knew who she was talking about, they'd probably think that she'd read about it in the paper and had imagined her part in it."

"What happens now?"

"They'll file a report with the D.C. cops," I replied. "In a few days somebody will come to talk to her."

"A policeman?"

"Yes."

Mary closed her eyes. When she opened them, she asked, "What now?"

"Get her out of here. Back to Ohio is best."

"Will she be safe there?"

I shook my head. "If you mean will she be out of reach of the police, no. But you might stand a better chance of keeping her from convicting herself."

She nodded her understanding. "My parents will have to know," she said.

I didn't reply. It was better that she work through that herself.

182

After a while she said, "It's time they did." She stood up and went to the telephone hanging on the kitchen wall. A telephone directory lay on the counter beneath the phone. She flipped its pages, found the number she wanted, and dialed. When she returned to the table, she had what she needed.

"We have reservations on a flight tomorrow morning," she said. "It's the earliest I could get."

"That should be soon enough," I assured her.

"I want to spend the night with you," she said. "There's so little time."

I went around the table and pulled her to me and kissed her. "There's no time," I said.

Her eyes questioned me. "Dan, what you said last night . . ."

"Yes. It's better that you are out of town too." I went and stood by the door.

Taffy had been waiting for me the night before. He could have seen her. He could have noted her car license number. By now he could know who she was and where she lived. It was a lot easier doing it that way than following me around.

"I'll come back," she promised.

Well, maybe she would and maybe she wouldn't. I hoped she would, but I doubted she'd stay. To her I was a door, too long closed, but now opened wide and showing her all the wonders on the other side. She couldn't just stand by the door and look at those wonders. She had to get out there and experience them.

She suggested another possibility. "Come with me," she said, almost coyly. "Why shouldn't I bring home a lover?" she asked.

I shook my head. "Someone killed Ted Fromann, and you hired me to find out who. I can't do that in Ohio."

Her face turned solemn. "Suppose," she began, "suppose that it really was Dilly?"

"Then we should know, shouldn't we?"

"Yes," she replied. "I'll have to call my parents and warn them. About Dilly."

We kissed at the door and then I went out of it, into the rain and down the steps, along the cracked sidewalk. The two of us never had gotten to the finish line. Something seemed to have been left hanging, but there wasn't anything else to say. I had the feeling that I'd been listening to a tantalizing melody and the tape had broken before it was over. And, no matter how short the song, you always want to be around for the ending.

184

16

THE NIGHT MAN had replaced Ralph in the lobby by the time I returned.

"Got something for you," he said, laying a plastic soup spoon beside a wide-mouthed thermos. Out of the thermos came the tantalizing aroma of homemade soup. I was glad I had stopped for dinner on my way back from Maryland.

The guard handed me a long, white envelope made out of that crinkly paper that looks as though you could print money on it. The envelope was addressed to me. No return address was on the envelope. "Guy in a chauffeur's uniform brought it in," said the guard. "He said it was important. That's all."

I took it and went up in the elevator. Inside my office I tossed my coat aside and sat down behind the desk and opened the envelope. The two sheets of good paper within were typed single-spaced. There was no letterhead. It started, "Cronyn," that was all. No signature, no other name. I didn't need a signature. I knew who had written it.

I stopped by your office a little past four with the intention of having you buy me the drink you owe me. Sorry I missed you.

I'm going home, Cronyn, to spare my government, my wife, and myself the embarrassment of discovery. You know what I did; nothing more needs to be said about it.

What I did not do, however, was commit any

185

other crime, specifically that of murder. I never knew the dead man nor of any connection he might have had with someone who was once very dear to me. You know who I mean.

Her husband is, as you know, behind the scheme. He approached me through one of my countrymen who was known in the Miami exile community for his success in living reasonably well without any visible means of support. I was asked, as a favor, to bring in a very small quantity of the material. Gradually the quantity grew; soon money was exchanged, a substantial amount of money for the amount of work required.

Why did I become involved? I wish I could remember. The easy answer is, naturally, the money. Who can't use a bundle of extra cash? But I suppose that it was also the mischievousness of it. You know, getting away with something.

It just occurred to me: what do you think my mother or wife would say if they were to find out what I was doing?

You had it right. I took the money down and brought the stuff back. The large lady distributes it through her girls. One thing you may not have known is that she sends the money back to the main man by way of the man's dear boy, whom you have met.

Dear boy also carries to the large lady the names and phone numbers of those individuals who've expressed an interest in making a connection with a dealer. It's very high-class all the way, like getting a new doctor when you move to another city.

The main man helps his friends in the government. In return, they help him. So far as I know, there's nothing illegal about what they do for him, but I am not an expert on your laws. The man would not, however, and understandably so, want his complete role exposed.

He could be a dangerous opponent, my friend. I hope you realize that and that you know what you are doing. If you are acting for the good of humanity, I wish I could have been in it with you instead of on the other side. We'd have made a pair. Two knights of yore to the rescue of the weak (and to the delight of the fair), buckling our swashes, and toppling the face of evil.

I'm sorry I could not help you when you asked for my help. Too much is at stake, too many innocent people would suffer if I were to expose myself.

However, I have warned my ex-colleague that I would return and expose him if harm should befall you. I've no doubt that he'll take that warning seriously. He knows that I can hurt him badly, even destroy him. That much, at least, I can do for you.

I wish that we had met sooner. We could have had a good drink or two, and a ball game, and a serious talk now and then, about women, about sports, about the Meaning of Life. We are much alike, I think, each alone in our own way.

A long life, my friend. Perhaps we shall meet again; perhaps not.

That was all.

I sailed the two sheets of paper gently onto the top of my desk and got up and went to the window and looked out at the darkness. Like I said, he could get under your skin, without ever knowing that he was doing it.

I didn't doubt he would do just what he had threatened to do if Devlin issued a contract on my life. Worse, I expected Devlin knew him well enough to take the threat seriously. Ramirez had set the seal to his own death warrant by associating himself with me.

187

I went to the file cabinet and put Scotch in a paper cup and took it back to the desk and raised it in a salute.

"Here's to your swash," I said aloud. "Good luck, pal."

I drank the whiskey in one swallow and sat down in my chair to think about the Meaning of Life and how to go about saving both of ours.

I closed the suitcase and put it on the floor beside the desk. It contained what I thought I'd need for a few days' stay at the Twenty Grand.

Maybe I was kidding myself about trying to keep up the pretense of remaining in business while being unable to use my own office. I looked around at the place. It wasn't much—the beat-up furniture, the files that represented dozens of forgotten people and their problems, also forgotten, the chalk drawings on the walls—not much at all.

But whatever it amounted to, it wouldn't fit into a suitcase.

I began unpacking, putting everything back where it all belonged. Very carefully. I cleared the top of the desk, straightened the pictures, adjusted the Venetian blinds so that they didn't hang crookedly. The cleaning people had been in earlier in the evening so the floor was swept and the wastebasket emptied.

The place suited me and, if a place suits you, you might as well die there as in a stranger's place.

The telephone rang. I went to the desk and sat down and picked up the receiver. If it was a stranger's voice, or no voice at all, I'd know what it meant, and I'd know what to do.

"Yes?" I said.

"Cronyn?" It was no stranger's voice. It was Paula Devlin's voice, and she sounded cross. "I've tried the number you gave me several times. You said you would be there."

"I had another errand. What is it?"

"I have to see you. I can't talk over the phone."

"Can you answer questions? Yes or no questions?" I asked. "Like, does it have to do with the cocaine?"

"Dammit," she said. "I don't want to play question games. Do you want me to help you or not?"

I sighed. "Okay. I'll . . ."

The sound of a key in the lock of the office door grabbed my attention. It looked as though I was about to receive a visitor. I eased open the upper drawer on the right side of my desk. I put my hand in and felt the cold metal of the thirty-year-old Smith and Wesson forty-four, guaranteed to knock the socks off unwanted intruders.

But it was only the downstairs guard. I took my hand out of the drawer.

He stood aside and allowed a familiar figure, short and solid, hands thrust deeply into the pockets of the same blue raincoat, to cross the threshold.

"Hello, cowboy," he said, showing his teeth. His eyes were chips of black granite.

"Hold on," I told the phone.

The guard went out and shut the door behind him, leaving Detective Paddock standing halfway between the door and my desk.

"I'm on my way out," I told him. "It's important."

"You ain't going nowhere, cowboy, until we have a little talk."

"Don't push me, Paddock. I'm not in the mood."

"Karle is downstairs with two uniformed officers. Make a break for it, Cronyn, and we'll use whatever force is required to take you into custody."

"For what?"

He just smiled. There was no humor in it. "Tell whoever it is that you'll get back to them. Sometime. After you and I clear up a few things."

Whatever it was he wanted obviously wasn't going to wait.

I spoke into the phone without taking my eyes off the police detective. "Something's come up." The one place I didn't want her was in my office. If Devlin were having it watched, she'd be seen, and if she were seen he would have his suspicions that we were working together confirmed. That would end her usefulness as a spy in the Devlin household. It might also end her.

"Okay," I told her, swiveling the chair away from Paddock. "Go to the motel. It's in Silver Spring. I'll meet you there, but I can't say when."

She didn't sound happy with such an open-ended appointment but in the end she agreed.

I hung up and swung around to face Paddock. "All right," I said.

He sat down in the chair opposite me. He smiled humorlessly, but didn't say anything.

"You wanted something?" I asked.

"Girlfriend?" inquired Paddock, indicating the phone.

"Client. Husband is giving her problems."

"Bet you get a lot of free snatch that way, don't you, cowboy?" Paddock grinned.

"You didn't come here to talk about my sex life."

The grin faded. "I hear you been taking an interest in Jacquie Germaine."

"My back's been bothering me recently. Only thing to fix it is a good rubdown."

"Still a smart-ass, huh, cowboy? Might be I'll have to fix that. Now let me ask you again. What about you and Jacquie?"

"Nothing about me and Jacquie."

"Then why the questions?"

That's the way they work you. They don't tell you anything. They just ask a lot of questions and wait for the lies. When they figure they have enough lies, they come at you, throwing them all back at you, making you want to tell the truth to get them off your case.

Paddock knew something, and I didn't know what it was. Maybe he'd had a whisper about where to go for some good stuff. He might have picked something up from the street. Then again, he might not. Devlin's operation, I guessed, was limited to people who didn't go to the street for their fixes.

"Friend of mine used Jacquie's professional services," I replied. "I just was interested in seeing that she ran a straightforward operation. No hidden cameras, that sort of thing."

That seemed to satisfy him. He took out his notebook and wrote it down. "What's the friend's name?"

"Can't tell you that, Detective Paddock."

He lay the notebook and his pen carefully on the edge of my desk. "I was kind of hoping that I was going to have trouble with you, cowboy."

"No trouble," I assured him.

"All right. You'll get all the breaks from me, Cronyn. If you cooperate. If not, well, that's more trouble than you can handle."

"What trouble?"

"Homicide, cowboy," he answered. "Somebody put the barrels of two guns in Jacquie's ears and pulled both triggers at once."

A nerve in my cheek twitched. At least I think it did. I hoped Paddock hadn't noticed.

He didn't seem to. "Guy stood over her and behind her. She was on her knees. Big guy, tall anyway. Not much left of her head but best we can tell is that the guns pointed down 'cause the guy was so tall."

I swallowed hard. "Sounds like an execution."

"Yeah. That's what I think. Almost like a drug thing. You know, where the big boys find somebody knocking down on them or maybe somebody with a loose mouth."

191

"She had a guy with her. Skinny, maybe thirty, thirty-five."

"Rail, everybody called him. Gone. Figure that he's worried that whoever got Jacquie wants him, too."

"You don't figure him to have killed her?"

"Huh-uh. Rail's been with her since he was a kid. Used to hold numbers for her. Only one to stay with her through the bad times. He's gone now, looking out for his own skin, I'd say."

"Where did she get it?" I asked.

"At the dump on Fourteenth. Rail probably found the body. We got an anonymous call shortly after six. Dispatcher remembers the dude was crying. He was long gone by the time we got there."

"No witnesses?"

"No," he replied. "Nobody heard anything. Nobody saw anything."

"That's the kind of neighborhood it is," I said.

"Yeah." He hitched himself up in the chair. "Place was a mess," he went on. "Somebody like to tear it apart. Whoever it was even unraveled the toilet paper in the john."

"Sounds like somebody was looking for something."

"It does, doesn't it? Whatta ya think it was, cowboy? I mean, you and Jacquie were getting pretty tight. Any idea what was in that dump that was worth all the exertion?"

"Incorrect premise, Detective Paddock," I said. I wanted to be polite. I wanted him to leave. If Paula Devlin had something for me, I wanted whatever she had. If she only had trouble, I needed to deal with it. What I didn't need was Paddock. But I had him, regardless. "Jacquie and I were not getting tight. I went to her place, like I said. That's all."

His black eyes glittered. "That's all," he repeated. "How about that? Know what her preacher told me happened today?" He didn't wait for my answer. "Seems a white man came to see Jacquie at her church about noon. Waited for her. Had words with her on the sidewalk. Jacquie even had to pull a gun on the guy to get away from him. The dude gave your name, cowboy. You better find out who's going around impersonating you."

I didn't say anything. Paddock had covered a lot of ground in the last couple of hours.

In any event he didn't seem to expect an answer. His lips flattened across his teeth. He showed me that sterile, wolfish grin.

"Whoever turned the place over," he went on, "probably didn't find what they were looking for. Same thing in Jacquie's apartment. A mess. Neighbors heard noises about seven-thirty, eight o'clock." He paused. "Guess what we found in the backroom of her massage parlor? Some plastic wrap and a heat-sealing machine. And some white dust in a drawer. Coke, cowboy, nose candy. But no stash. Where do you suppose it got to?"

"Not here," I told him. "What about her girls?"

He slouched back in the chair, his neck beginning to recede into his collar.

"We rounded up all the girls. Only five of them. None of them know anything, so they claim. We'll see." He sized me up with his black granite eyes. "You're a big motherfucker," he said. "Tall enough to fit the bill."

"I have an alibi."

"Tell me about it."

"My lawyer does the talking for me."

"Who you working for, Cronyn?"

"Ask my lawyer."

"You hire out to dope dealers to eliminate their problems?"

"I don't carry a gun."

"What about the forty-four in the upper right-hand drawer?"

I'd almost forgotten he'd been in my office a few days earlier.

"Maybe Jacquie found out something that worried her," said Paddock. "She was always a cautious one. She could have called your boss and told him she wanted out."

I let him speculate.

"The boss could have sent you around," he continued, "to find out how much she'd already talked and to who. You put her on her knees and told her to spill it all or get blown to hell. She spills and gets blown to hell anyway."

"That's all blue smoke, Paddock. You know that."

"Do I? Tell yourself what I know, cowboy. Last Monday I find you standing over the body of somebody else who got in the way of a lot of bullets."

"I'm not a trigger man."

"All right. Set-up man then. What's his name—Fromann—is expecting you bringing cash, only it's the hit man who shows up. Same's with Jacquie. She's expecting you, gets the guy with two automatics instead."

I stood up. "I've been fingerprinted before. Let's go talk to a judge."

"Sure. So you can hand him that fairy tale about the woman who paid you to buy letters from Fromann or the one about your pal getting blowed at Jacquie's place."

Then he stood up, too. Only he didn't move toward the door. He came toward me, around the desk, his hands out of his pockets.

This time it was no surprise. I saw it coming. Maybe he thought that the fear of his badge would keep me paralyzed. He was wrong.

I deflected his punch with my left arm and threw my own solid, satisfying right, which caught him on the mouth. It threw his head back. He staggered backwards and went down on one knee.

"Get out of here, Paddock." My breath was coming fast.

He shook his head, trying to clear it. He stayed down on that one knee for a double count.

I gave him a chance to recover and to stand. I wished I hadn't.

He had his gun in his hand. It pointed to my abdomen from a distance of four feet.

"Thanks," he said. Blood ran down his chin from his mouth. He didn't bother to wipe it away. "Both hands on the desk, facing forward. This is going to be fun."

"No way, Paddock. You're not going to work me over."

"No? Try this, cowboy. I'm trying to take you into custody. You attack me. I try to fight you off but you go for my gun. In the struggle, the gun goes off." He spat out a broken tooth. "There's all the evidence I need, smart-ass. You gonna be dead. Only one of us to say what happened."

His lips stretched flat across his teeth. His eyes, no longer cold, no longer small, glowed hotly, round and wide. Paddock wanted to shoot someone. It looked like I had just won the prize.

I put my hands out from my body, palms down. "Okay, okay. I shouldn't have hit you. It was stupid and bad judgment. You got me for assaulting an officer in the line of duty. Let's go downstairs to the cruiser."

Let's go anywhere, I was thinking, to break that crazed circuit which had connected in his head.

He wasn't listening. "I'm going to hurt you, boy. You're like all the other smart-ass street fuckers. But when you're hurt you won't be such a smart . . ."

"Paddock."

A new voice cracked across the room from the doorway. As Paddock and I had done our slow-motion dance of death, we had turned so that the door was behind me.

I didn't look around to see the newcomer. I kept my eyes on Paddock.

He looked toward the door. Surprise crossed his face.

"Holster your piece," ordered the new voice.

The surprise faded from Paddock's face. Dogged resolve replaced it. "Stay out of it, Rowlson. This is my arrest."

The other man moved further into the room. He stood beside me.

"You will obey a direct order, Detective, or I will have your gun and your badge," he said.

Anger blazed in Paddock's eyes. The gun drifted a bit toward the newcomer, "Fuck off, Lieutenant. This lying cock-sucker isn't getting out of this one."

"As of this moment, Paddock, you're on administrative leave. You have no more right to be holding that gun than any street punk."

Silence. All I could hear was the sound of heavy breathing. I think it was mine.

Paddock's eyes changed. He stared at the man beside me. Grinding into place behind his eyes were the years of training, practice, and discipline that had gone into him. A war was going on in his mind, a war between those years and the hate and rage that had built up in him over the futility of his job.

The war ended. Discipline won. I suspected that we'd have all died if it had not.

Paddock looked at the gun in his hand as though it belonged to someone else. "Sure, Lieutenant. Sure." He started to replace it inside his coat. He stopped, visibly changing his mind. "Here, Lieutenant. You keep it." He handed it, grip first, to Rowlson.

Rowlson put it in his topcoat pocket. "Wait for me downstairs," he said.

I stood aside and let Paddock go past. At the door stood a white-faced Detective Karle. Beyond, in the hall, two uniformed officers waited.

Paddock stopped at the door and faced Karle. "You did it, didn't you? You called the Lieutenant."

196

"Look, Paddy . . ."

"Shut up. You can't do nothing worse than fuck your own partner. You know that, but you did it anyway. You're nothing but a piece of shit, Karle."

Paddock pushed his way through the door leaving Karle with his jaw working, wanting to say something.

I figured he needed a word of comfort from the man whose life he'd saved. "Thanks, Detective Karle."

He stared at me, his face dead white, the corners of his mouth turned down. "I didn't do it for you," he said. "Hell, I did it for him."

Rowlson dismissed him and faced me. "It'll be as hard on Paddock as you want to make it." He was the same tall, slender chestnut-skinned cop who had come to Fromann's apartment.

"Good." I went to the file cabinet and took out the bottle. My hands shook a little. If you face a man who seems half-nuts and he's pointing a gun at you, there's going to be a reaction. I guarantee it.

"Al Paddock was a good officer once," Rowlson said.

"Bring out the violins and flowers."

Rowlson took a deep breath. "We've got psychiatrists . . . ," he began.

"Look, Lieutenant. I appreciate your saving my life, but sending Paddock back on the street is playing with dynamite." I poured some whiskey into my paper cup and drank it.

"He won't go back on the street. There are other jobs. Administration, training. We could find a place for him. Or we could destroy him."

I put the paper cup down on the desk. "Jesus Christ, that's good, coming from a cop. What about justice? Isn't that what you guys are always talking about?"

Rowlson hunched his shoulders. He looked cold. "You're right, Mr. Cronyn. Good night." He turned to go.

I wasn't about to let him have the last word. "When it comes to the hearing, though, none of this will have happened, right, Lieutenant?"

He turned back to me, his eyes hot. "I'm going to get Al Paddock off the street, Cronyn, before he kills somebody. I don't want to have to take police work away from him. I don't want to destroy him. But if that's what it takes, I'm going to do it."

He started to leave again. Something stopped him. "His wife left a couple of years ago to shack up with a street pusher from Philly driving a white Caddy. His kid doesn't come home from school, thinks it's fun to hang out on the street. Thinks guys like his mother's lover have it all together. Thinks his old man is some kind of jerk." He stopped abruptly, almost as though he were looking back at something.

Justice comes in strange packages. I'd be the first to give a street punk who might go straight the break he needed. I wondered why it was so hard for me to see behind Paddock's badge to the man who wore it. I wondered why I didn't even want to look.

There are times when I wish I still retained the assumed certainties of my salad days. I didn't ask for all these damned questions. They just pop up when I least expect them. I'd been perfectly happy with the image of Paddock as the arrogant, brutal cop, which he was. That hadn't changed. But then, all of a sudden the image you've been so comfortable with lets you hear its voice and sometimes that voice has agony and pain and despair in it, and you have to look at yourself and wonder if you even know yourself, let alone the other guy.

Rowlson walked to the door. I stopped him.

"You think your shrink can help Paddock?" I asked his back.

He turned. "I think it's worth a try."

"Then I figure he and I are even," I said.

198

He took a moment to digest that. Then, "Thanks, Cronyn. Somebody will be in touch to get a statement from you about the case he was working on, the Germaine homicide," Rowlson said.

"I'm not going anywhere."

"Yeah," he hesitated as though he wanted to say something but didn't know how to do it without it coming out sounding stupid. So he just said, "See you later, Cronyn."

"Right, Lieutenant."

I turned the lights off and sat for a few minutes in the dark thinking about what Paddock had told me. When I felt sure that I had it all right, I stood up, knowing what to do.

Paula Devlin would keep. She had too much at stake to go far.

I left the office one minute later, carrying the empty canvas suitcase in my left hand and the full forty-four in my jacket pocket.

17

I CROSSED THE pavement quickly. The street lights showed grotesquely through the bare limbs and branches of the trees that lined both sides of the street. The rain had stopped.

Nothing moved. Even the wind seemed at rest. The moon glowed feebly behind the spire that loomed ahead of me. A halo circled the moon and seemed to circle the top of the church as well. It gave the building a look of eerie sanctity.

The houses on this all-black, all–middle-class street, were dark, their occupants gathering their strength for the day to come, safe in the comfort of their beds on this long winter's night.

But I went fast up the concrete steps with the steel pipe railing. Reduced to burglarizing a house of worship was bad enough; getting caught at it would have been much worse.

The big main doors in front were locked. I had expected it. I had come prepared to pick a lock, but not that one. I needed a door to the rear or side, one where I could work briefly over the lock with my penlight strapped to my wrist. I needed a door that was somewhat removed and hidden from the street.

I found it on the right side of the church, near the rear corner.

The church was built as a split level. That is, the front of the church where the worship went on was one story.

In the rear, it was two stories. Outside, brick steps went up to the upper story and down into a basement.

I chose the basement door. It was hidden behind the steps, giving me plenty of cover.

I took my lock-picking set from my coat pocket and shone the light on the lock. It didn't look too difficult. I gave a tentative tug on the door to make certain of its ease and direction of swing.

It opened.

I stood there for three seconds comtemplating the opening before I slipped the fold-over tool kit back into my pocket and followed the beam of my light through the door. I shut it silently after me.

A lingering smell of disinfectant hung in the still air. The light revealed that asphalt tile covered a concrete floor. Simple tubular steel tables and folding chairs were scattered around a large, open room. Some sort of recreation area, I decided, complete with kitchen.

The light picked out stairs. I went up. I stopped on a landing midway and shone the light upward. The head of the stairway opened to a hall going across the width of the church, probably connecting the meeting rooms, Sunday School and the like.

What I was looking for, what I'd hoped to find, wasn't likely to be up there.

The door beside me led to the pews, I figured. I eased my thumb away from the switch on the penlight. Total darkness surrounded me. Until I was sure of where I stood once past that door, I didn't want the light to be caught by one of the large, outside windows.

I eased the door open and slipped through. The air inside was dry and still. An odor I hadn't expected threaded its way past my nose.

A sound. Off to my right. A scuffling sound. Four yards beyond me, maybe twice that far.

I hadn't expected the Eternal Glory of God Temple to have mice.

But mice don't drink beer, at least not enough of it to leave such a heavy smell of the stuff in that hanging air.

I still held the penlight in my left hand. My right went inside my raincoat to the forty-four in my jacket pocket. You'd know why I don't very often carry a gun if you lugged that thing around for a while.

For this excursion, I had thought of the psychological comfort it provided, however, and brought it along. I was glad I did.

I pointed the penlight and the gun in the direction of the sound and pressed the light switch.

The beam made it just far enough for me to see the white sweater. He was standing, rigid, about a third of the way back from the front of the church, between the rows of pews, close to the far wall.

It was kind of a sob that came out of him. "Oh Jesus," he cried.

I moved closer to get a better look at him.

His eyes bulged. He made motions with his hands as though he were trying to push the light away.

"Oh Jesus, oh Jesus, oh Jesus," he moaned.

He staggered and nearly fell down. Drunk. Plastered to the gills. And scared shitless. Literally.

A new odor assailed my nostrils. I stopped my forward motion.

"Rail," I said. "It's Cronyn."

He moaned some more. I repeated what I said. He blubbered something about Jacquie, about her having no face. He slumped down on the hard pew behind him and moaned, slobbering out his fear of death.

"Rail," I repeated. His eyes rolled upward, unable to focus, glassy in the beam of the flashlight. "Who killed her?"

A tiny stream of saliva crept down from one corner of his mouth. He shook his head. One hand waved in the air as though it were disconnected from the rest of him.

I repeated my question.

"Oh, man," he moaned. His eyes stared into the darkness in panic. "Don't let him in." He was babbling now. "Please. He hurt Jacquie. Oh, God. She should have taught me how to pray. He won't get me here, will he?" His eyes pleaded for reassurance.

"Who, Rail? Dammit, who?"

His eyes rolled. "The queen," he said. "The big fucking queen. He came to see Jacquie. Said he had a message. He told me to get lost."

"Who was the message from?"

He wobbled his head drunkenly. "The connection."

"Who's the connection? Does he have a name?"

The head wobbled again. "Doan know. Just the connection."

His head wobbled again, signifying his uselessness as a witness against Devlin, even in the unlikely event that he could be persuaded to talk. And that assumed he'd still be alive when the cops found him, a dubious assumption at best. Taffy might have second thoughts about leaving someone around who could talk about his visit to Jacquie Germaine.

"Did Jacquie want out?"

The drunken motion of his head became more of a nod. His hand crept out from his side along the bench. I saw it because I wasn't taking any chances with Rail, even as plastered as he was.

The beam of my penlight followed his groping hand. Four or five cans of beer sat on the bench next to him. He took one, popped its cap and gurgled a lot of it down, some of it escaping his mouth to end up dripping from his chin.

204

He wiped his mouth with his sleeve. "She didn't want to be messed up in a killing," he said.

"Whose killing?"

He looked at me with strange eyes, as though he had just discovered who he was talking to. It didn't take many smarts to conclude whose murder Jacquie wanted to stay out of.

Mine.

Devlin had sent Taffy to let Jacquie know who was in charge, probably. Taffy would likely have had orders from his boss to be sure of her, or else. Taffy is a tough man to persuade, as I knew, and his preference always seemed to be for the "or else." I wondered how hard Jacquie had begged, on her knees, feeling the hard, cold steel of Taffy's pistols pressing against her eardrums.

Not hard enough. She probably never heard the explosions that blew out her brains. The last thing she'd have heard was Taffy's little giggle of pleasure. Beautiful Taffy, at play.

"You went back?" I asked Rail.

His head bobbled forward.

"And?"

"The queen's gone, and Jacquie's on the floor in the office." He stared at his can of beer blankly, all the horror coming back to him. "She's got no face. Oh, God a-mighty," he moaned and swayed on his seat.

I stood there for the space of several breaths before moving away, leaving him in the dark, alone, while I went looking for the spot where I remembered seeing Jacquie Germaine at prayer. I hoped that it would do her some good now, in whatever place her immortal soul had been called to.

As for Rail, he was beyond interfering with what I had come to do. A cocoon of fear enveloped him, terrifying him beyond reason.

Most of the benches in the church had square boxes with padded tops under them. The boxes were sturdy dark pine about twenty inches by twelve inches by nine inches deep. Some had names on them. Some didn't. I supposed that a kneeling box with your name on it came with a substantial donation to the church.

Jacquie had been kneeling near the outside end of one of the aisles. Not the exact end, just close. I knew I had the proper row when I spied kneeling boxes with the name Germaine on them. There were two of them.

I sat on the bench approximately where I had seen her. I leaned forward and pulled the kneeling box directly in front of me into the space between my bench and the back of the bench ahead of me. I knelt down on its padded top, assuming the same prayerful position I had seen Jacquie in.

The other box with the name Germaine, the one at the extreme end of the row, was bigger than the others and wouldn't budge, despite my efforts at pulling it. I figured that I had found what I had come looking for.

I looked for movement in the top of it or along its sides without success. I worked at it for ten minutes, sweating in the cold, dark church.

A sound startled me. I turned off the penlight and grabbed the forty-four from the bench beside me. I listened, hardly daring to take a breath.

The sound came again, steadier now. I used the light once more to check on Rail. He slept peacefully, curled on the hard bench. The line of saliva dripping from his open mouth formed a tiny pool on the polished wood. His fingers clasped an open can of beer, holding it at a cock-eyed angle.

He snored. That was the sound I had heard. The alcohol had finally conquered wakefulness and fear.

I couldn't take all night. Devlin wouldn't be waiting for his contract killer from Miami. He and Taffy would have to take care of me themselves. And soon. I had no desire to be trapped in that church by them.

The coat interfered with my mobility so it went on the bench beside the gun. I pushed the movable kneeling box out of the way and lay on the floor.

Another ten minutes gave me the answer to the box. There were two hidden spring latches which had to be operated simultaneously and the top of the box swung, rather than lifted or slid.

I'd found it. Jacquie's cache. The reason for her to visit the church nearly every day. The reason for pulling a gun on me when I inadvertently grabbed the canvas bag she carried. The reason Paddock's men found no cocaine at Jacquie's office.

I lifted from the cache the first of the many clear plastic bags of snow-white powder that it contained.

I drove to Virginia immediately after leaving the church. The canvas suitcase on the seat behind me contained clear plastic bags of cocaine, twenty-three of them, each weighing, I guessed, a pound or a little more, maybe half a kilo, all that had been in Jacquie's secret storage.

After thinking about it for a while, it made sense that Jacquie would not keep all her stock at the massage parlor. To begin with, the place wasn't too secure and people who knew she was dealing might figure to burgle the place and get a free high. Lots and lots of free highs. Or resell the stuff.

She also wouldn't want to sit on the stuff at the most obvious place for the cops to come to. That was too big a chance for getting caught with it. Jacquie had been too cautious to take that risk.

The logical thing for her to do was to keep it in an unlikely place, which place she could visit daily without anyone paying any particular attention. That way she could take a bag or two of the cocaine—whatever she had orders for that day—to the place on 14th and repackage just what she expected to give to her girls for delivery.

When Taffy had not been able to find the main cache at the massage parlor after killing her, he must have gone to her apartment. After not finding it there either, he'd have reported to Devlin. Eventually Devlin would come to the same conclusion that I had come to.

But I had gotten there first.

I went to an all-night drug and two twenty-four hour supermarkets before I found what I needed.

I parked the station wagon under a lamppost at the end of the last supermarket's parking lot and went to work. I lifted the tailgate open and sat the suitcase on the floor at the end of the hatch. I arranged my purchases—Scotch tape, cardboard stencil letters, and a can of black spray paint beside it. I used the Scotch tape to hold selected stencil letters on the side of the large, canvas suitcase, as straight as I could manage. I squirted the area with the black aerosol paint, the quick-drying kind. I peeled off tape and letters and considered the result and found it acceptable.

Major Rogers had just returned from overseas.

The night clerk in the transient apartment building gave only a quick glance at the name and rank stenciled in black on the side of the military-looking suitcase. He wanted to go back to sleep, so when I gave him the story about the long day I'd had and about just getting in from Frankfurt and all the rest, he handed me the key to Paula Devlin's apartment and forgot me.

I went up and took the mattress off the bed and spread the bags of cocaine evenly across the box spring. The mattress went back on top, and then the sheets and

208

blanket and spread. A neatly made bed. A half-million-dollar bed.

If Devlin wanted his coke, all he had to do was come and get it. The important thing was that when I called Devlin and made my deal and told him to meet me there, it would be cops he met and not me.

For as hard as Devlin had worked to keep the dope at arm's length, he was finally going to be caught with the stuff on him.

I arrived at the Twenty Grand a little after two in the morning. The parking lot was less than a third full. Christmas isn't the best time for the Twenty Grand except early in the evenings when the couples who connect at the office parties need a bed.

I sat in the car for a moment surveying the quiet motel. The only light I saw, except in the office, was a dim line along the lower edge of the window in twenty-two, at the end of the one-story building. I slid out of the car and walked across the black-topped parking lot.

I tapped lightly on the door. It opened almost immediately. Paula Devlin stood there. She must have been watching for me. She moved back to let me enter.

"Had a couple of errands," I explained stepping into the room. That's when everything began to go wrong.

The door slammed behind me.

Devlin came out of the bathroom in front of me, tapping the end of a cigarette against his gold case.

"Take his gun, Taffy," he commanded.

18

ONE OF THE other reasons I seldom carry a gun is that I'm sure it'll never do me any good when I really need it. Like right then. It was in my pocket.

Taffy ordered me out of the lined raincoat and patted me down with one large, yet delicate, hand.

"He's getting a cheap feel," I said to Devlin. My reward for trying to lighten the occasion was a vicious chop at the kidney. I went down on hands and knees feeling sick.

Taffy then drove his shoe against my right elbow. Pain arched from wrist to shoulder. The right arm no longer supported me so I tumbled onto my right side. My head cracked against the foot of the bed.

I rolled onto my back to see Taffy grinning down at me. He held a gun in his left hand and another materialized in his right. Both looked like cannons from that angle. Both were automatics. Both had suppressors on their barrels.

Devlin ordered me to sit on the bed. He had my gun, and he was lighting a cigarette, which he managed by flicking his lighter with one gloved hand while holding my pistol in the other.

"You should have left town when you had the chance," he told me, expelling smoke.

"In view of the current circumstances," I said, "you're absolutely right. Why don't I pack and leave now?" I hooked a thumb toward Taffy. "He can drive me to the airport and see that I get on a plane."

A cold smile flickered across Devlin's face. "Too late," he said.

"I see," I said. "The sandman is on his way from Miami to put me to sleep. Or are you planning a do-it-yourself job?"

"I can't afford to allow you to run loose. Taffy and I will handle it." He puffed again. "After all, it's not like we had to go and find you and try to maneuver you into position."

"Yeah. You've already maneuvered me." I looked at Paula Devlin. "With help."

"Yes. My dear treasonous wife hoped to return to favor in my household."

Paula Devlin cast a sharp look toward her husband. Something in his tone worried her.

"She said," continued Devlin, "that you had forced her to cooperate with you under the threat of revealing a previous love affair. You wanted her to report to you on the whereabouts of merchandise belonging to me. She leaped at the chance to lead you into this delightfully simple situation."

I looked at his wife. "It'll be a murder rap," I said.

She turned her face away from me.

Devlin spoke. "I don't believe she likes you, Cronyn."

Taffy giggled behind me. He was on a roll. He didn't like me either, and it looked as though he was going to have the chance to do something about it.

Devlin continued. "It will be a classic murder-suicide," he said. "You'll shoot her and then yourself."

Paula Devlin gasped and turned quickly toward her husband. "Walter," she said. "You can't. That's bizarre. That's . . ."

He cut her off, his voice hard. "You pursue your own interests too much, Paula. Your relations with this man have led me into great difficulty. Furthermore, I have no doubt that you would have cooperated fully with Cronyn

212

if it had not been for some reason of your own to want him out of the picture." He snuffed out his cigarette. "Taffy was right all along about you." He raised my gun in her direction.

"My God, Walter," she said, her voice strangling with fear. Her face was ashen.

"There's one more thing, Devlin, "I interjected. "It's important."

He held the gun up, still pointed at her, but he glanced in my direction, mildly curious.

"I have the coke," I said. "All of it."

The gun wavered slightly. "That's impossible."

"Why? Just because you didn't know where Jacquie kept it?"

"Her office was searched thoroughly."

"So the cops told me. Saved me the trouble of looking."

Delvin smiled again. "A nice try, Cronyn. But we went to her apartment before anyone else."

"You must have been pretty desperate by that time."

Devlin narrowed his eyes and lowered the gun to his waist. Paula swayed slightly. "You're bluffing," said Devlin.

"A bluff wouldn't work if you had the stuff."

"That doesn't mean that you have it," he countered.

"Taffy assumed that she kept it in her office. Big mistake. Too late to fix after she was dead."

He thought that one over, trying to assess my veracity.

Paula, still sitting on the bed beside me, was breathing as though she had just run up five flights of stairs. She tried to talk to her husband.

"Walter," she said, "anything you want. My only interests are yours." She had to take a breath. "Walter, please. I brought him here."

"Shut up," he replied. Of me he asked, "Where is it, Cronyn?" His voice was raw with menace.

"No good, Walter. If I tell you, then we both know, and you don't need me."

He raised my gun and sighted along it to my forehead. "You have thirty seconds to make up your mind."

He knew what he was doing, all right. Five seconds or even ten seconds was too short a time to really think about dying. Thirty seconds seemed like an eternity.

Our eyes met and locked. Sweat dripped from my armpits. My mouth filled with cotton. He'd break me if I just sat there thinking about what it was like taking a bullet in the brain.

"For that kind of a threat to work," I said, "I have to think that you'd rather see me dead than have your cocaine back. I don't."

"You could be wrong."

"Then we'd both be losers."

He lowered the forty-four. He smiled. "A good point," he conceded. "If you have the merchandise."

"I have it."

"You ask me to believe that in order to protect yourself. Self-serving statement, Cronyn. Where is your proof?"

"You'll have to take my word for it."

"Less than satisfactory, Cronyn. Much less than satisfactory. The trust in that arrangement is all on one side."

I wished I could have told him to look into the zippered lining of my raincoat where I had thoughtfully stashed a sample bag out of Jacquie's cache. Only I had not done that. Hadn't even thought of it, as a matter of fact.

"I don't think," Devlin went on, "that I believe you."

"Which makes it dangerous for me. If you don't believe I can produce the stuff, then there's nothing to stop you from shooting me."

"Exactly."

"Believe this then. Somebody had to keep the stuff and repackage it into customer-sized batches. Ramirez

214

delivered it to Jacquie, and her girls delivered it to the customers. If you put grass into one end of a cow and get milk out the other, you have to figure that whatever happened to the grass, happened inside the cow."

Taffy made a noise. I looked toward the door where he still stood. Only one of the cannons pointed in my direction. The other hung loosely at the end of his arm, pointing toward the floor. He was just giving the muscles in that arm a rest. Even prizefighters get to rest their arms every three minutes and they aren't holding two and a half pounds of iron at the end of them.

I turned back to Devlin. "Jacquie had a reputation for caution, for always leaving herself an out with the law. She'd try to minimize the risk of sitting on that much cocaine. So she'd keep it someplace other than her office or home, someplace she visited almost daily without suspicion."

"Where is this place?" asked Devlin.

"Her church."

He stared at me for the space of two breaths. "I see." He moved away from the door to the bathroom and went to sit in the room's one easy chair, in the corner facing Paula and me and the door.

He pushed my pistol down between the arm of the chair and its seat cushion. "And you found the material there."

"That's right."

"And took it away."

"Yes."

"And where is it now?" he asked.

"Safe. For the moment, anyway."

"I see." He put his hands together and manipulated his knuckles. "Does my dear wife know where it is?"

"No," I replied but he wasn't satisfied with that.

"Do you, my dear?"

"Of course not, Walter." She hesitated, not looking at

me. "I could go and search his office while you and Taffy keep him here."

He looked at me. "My wife is most helpful, wouldn't you say? Out of desperation, naturally."

"With good reason," I said. "She has an idea."

"Yes," he replied. "To save herself. Once out of this room, I doubt that we should ever see her again."

I shrugged. "Okay. So we're all here. You've got me, and I've got the merchandise. I won't tell you where it is because you'll shoot me after that."

A long silence followed while Devlin considered his alternative. I didn't think Devlin would give up the cocaine by shooting the one person in the room who knew where it was. On the other hand, I couldn't be sure. He had to consider me a threat to him because of what I knew.

Taffy stood a little to my right and behind me. I turned a little toward him. He raised the two large automatics. They looked even larger because of their noise suppressors. Bullets from those guns would make a mess of the human body. You could ask Rail about that. He'd seen what was left of Jacquie Germaine.

Devlin snuffed out his cigarette. He had come to a decision. He had no intention of losing the cocaine.

He ignored Paula and Taffy to look at me. "We shall go for it, all of us together."

I didn't like it and told him so. He didn't care what I liked. "Taffy," he said. "That woman's name, please."

Taffy answered, happily. "Mary Thresher. She lives with her sister in Maryland. The sister is some kind of retard."

Devlin looked at me while he gave Taffy his orders. "Do you think you can make her scream?"

"Devlin . . . ," I began.

He gave me a choice. I could witness Mary's torture

and then get bullets in the ears, or I could take them to the cocaine.

I took them, even offering to drive.

Taffy and I went up in the elevator to the fourth-floor apartment. My hands were in my pockets. One of Taffy's irons probed my ribs. My gun stayed behind in the motel.

We'd left Paula and Walter Devlin in the parking lot, sitting in my car. He had obtained one of Taffy's automatics and kept his wife covered with it.

Taffy and I exited the elevator and marched down the deserted hall. I used the key I had obtained earlier to let us in. I flipped the wall switch, and the table lamps came on. I stepped inside. Taffy came after me.

"Where is it?" he asked.

"In the bedroom."

"You first. Turn the lights on before going into any room. Take it easy. No sweat so far. If the stuff's here, you're home free."

That had been the promise. Deliver the goods, Cronyn, and you're home free. I don't think that I'd have believed it even if Devlin hadn't taken Taffy aside for a little tête-à-tête before leaving the Twenty Grand. Delvin didn't strike me as a man who liked leaving loose ends, and I felt like the loosest end that had ever gone unsnipped.

I led Taffy to the bedroom, adhering closely to his instructions.

"Under the mattress," I said.

He ordered me onto a chair in the corner of the room. He kept his eyes on me while he used his free hand to throw back the bedclothes and feel under the mattress. The expression on his pretty face gave away the contact his groping hand made with smooth plastic.

I slid forward on the chair so that my feet would be

under my center of gravity. Nothing could be done as long as Taffy faced me and pointed his cannon at me. If I intended to do anything, though, I couldn't wait until he became certain that he had accomplished the first half of his mission. Then he would concentrate on the second half. Me.

He should have had to squat down and reach farther and farther under the mattress to extract all the bags. That might have given me the opening I needed.

It didn't happen. What happened was that he used his free hand to flip the mattress off the bed while he looked at me. It landed with a thud against the floor on the other side of the bed.

My opportunity came so fast that it almost flew past without my taking advantage of it.

Taffy turned away for an instant to look at the cache of cocaine he had uncovered. My legs uncoiled, propelling me out of the chair and into a dive. My shoulder caught him in the gut. He grunted satisfactorily.

I also tried grabbing for his gun hand in my dive, but he must have sensed me coming. Instinctively he pulled his elbow closer to his body. It cracked against my head, and sharp pain blazed through my skull, illuminating little patches of multicolored light behind my eyes.

The collision between head and elbow, however, dislodged the gun from his suddenly nerveless fingers. It spun out of his hand, hit the polished parquet floor and finished up somewhere out of sight under the bed.

He kept his feet under him and twisted as I tried forcing him forward onto the bed. He took a grip on my left wrist with his good hand and tried to pull me around him to the bed using his twisting motion as leverage and his body as the axis of rotation.

I wanted none of his viselike grip. I'd been through that before. I pounded his right ear with my fist, persuad-

218

ing him to let go of my wrist. I hit him again, in the ribs, and stepped back, away from his powerful grasp.

We faced each other. Both of us breathed heavily. I faked a right, faded left, and connected on his jaw with the right. It was a solid hit, but it didn't stop him.

He took my left arm, bent it over his and got his hip behind me. Then he took me over it.

I hit the floor with a crash. A sharp pain raced through the first part of me to hit, my shoulder. A micro-second later, my head, following my shoulder, cracked on the parquet. Bright lights filled the interior, and the next thing I was conscious of was of him dragging me, only semi-conscious, to my feet.

He was breathing heavily and grinning. This was work Taffy enjoyed. I suspected Taffy would rather beat someone to death, even at the cost of a few bruises himself, than use the guns.

He reached for the back of my head with his left hand. He raised the other arm parallel to his shoulder and cocked his elbow. He wanted my face in just the right position when smashing it with that elbow.

I went in close, a dangerous thing to do with him. It meant that I was inside the circumference of his powerful arms. I had no choice. It was the only direction open to me.

My left caught him in the diaphragm. It gave him something else to think about. I tried to give him another something else to think about with a follow-up right to the mouth but I was in too close, and besides, my right shoulder wasn't working the way it should.

I backpedaled and wound up in the corner. He came after me, grinning. He sensed victory, was as sure of it as I was sure that I couldn't backpedal any further. I wouldn't wait for him to finish me off on his terms. He'd have to do it on mine.

I moved in with my head down. I clasped my hands together in a doubled fist. I let it hang between my knees, arms straining.

The aggressiveness surprised him. I felt his hands grabbing at me for a quick hold and toss. Before he realized what was happening, it was too late.

My head touched his chest. I straightened with a jerk, swinging my doubled fist up between his legs, crushing his testicles into his crotch. At the same time my head drove against his jaw, shutting off any yelp that he might have felt rising from the sickness and pain in his belly.

I fell back against the wall and fought back the deep black well of unconsciousness that I saw waiting for me. My knees sagged, my eyes unfocused. In a blur I saw Taffy on his knees with his hands tucked between his pressed thighs, bowing and moaning.

The gun. I had to reach the gun. Then it would end. I'd kill him if I had to, but first I had to have the gun. I staggered to the foot of the bed and went down on my knees.

He saw, out of glazed eyes, what I was doing. Sounds gurgled through wet lips.

No gun. I couldn't see it. I crawled to the other side of the bed, where he'd flipped the mattress.

I heard him. He was moving, despite his pain. He was coming for me.

He was on the bed, towering over me.

I dragged myself upward, going for him. We collided and he stepped backward. His foot disappeared, and he lurched sideward and as our bodies met he went backward, screaming in sudden agony as his leg, trapped between the bed frame and the springs, cracked.

I went past him onto the floor, turned and pushed myself up once more.

His eyes stared at me, bright with fear and pain. He opened his mouth. Blood and a piece of tooth came out.

"Help me," he managed to say. "Jesus, Jesus, get my leg out of there."

He'd tried to kill me, not just because he had to, but because he wanted to. He could have lain there like an animal in a leg-trap, except that I don't believe anybody should have to suffer like that. Not when I could do something about it, at any rate.

There wasn't much I could do at first but get the rest of his massive body back up on the bed. That gave him some relief. The next thing was to get his trapped leg out of the bed.

I didn't get far.

19

"Hold it right there, Cronyn," said the voice from the doorway.

I straightened up slowly from trying to engineer Taffy's leg up onto the bed with the rest of him. He'd lost consciousness from the pain, I guessed.

Devlin stood in the doorway. He pushed his wife off to the side of the room. He pointed Taffy's other gun at me and gave quick glances to Taffy and the havoc we'd created in the room, things you don't notice after the first collisions. The chair from which I'd launched my attack no longer existed. Scattered kindling lay near the spot where it had been. A mirror had shattered, lamps were destroyed. I couldn't remember any of it happening.

"He's hurt," I said. "We have to get his leg out of there and straighten it out. He could be bleeding."

He thought about something before replying. "Stand aside," he ordered finally. I did, persuaded by the gun pointed at me. He moved sideways to the bed, never taking his eyes from me. He searched Taffy with one hand. When he did not find what he was looking for, he asked, "Where's his gun?"

"I don't know."

He raised his gun to shoulder level and aimed. "Give it to me."

"If I had it, Walter, you'd be roasting on the devil's spit by now."

A cold, little smile played around his lips. He lowered the gun to hip level once more. His eyes flicked toward the mound of cocaine on the bed, but not for long enough to give me an opening even if I had been up to it. "Thank you, Cronyn. Now, help Taffy disentangle himself from his clumsy predicament, and we shall be on our way with the merchandise."

"And Mrs. Devlin and I?" I asked him.

"Taffy will see to it that you two are made comfortable."

Paula stepped forward from her position along the wall to my left. Her eyes looked scared but no longer panicked. "You have your material," she reminded him.

"Yes," he agreed. "Now I must have your silence. Stand closer to your partner, my dear wife."

She started to speak again, to make a protest. Taffy moaned as he regained consciousness.

"Get up Taffy," his boss ordered. "We must be on our way." He waved the automatic toward me. "Get over there, Paula, or I shan't wait until Taffy gets his oafish self off the bed."

She came close to me. I spoke to Devlin. "He's hurt, Devlin."

Taffy managed to grit out to his boss, "It's my leg, Walter. I can't move it. I . . ." That's all he could manage. After that he moaned obscenities and prayers mixed together in a litany of pain.

"Put down the gun, Devlin. Between the three of us it won't be any problem to get him to the hospital. Like your wife said, you have your stuff."

"No. You are too much of a threat."

"Walter, please . . . ," Taffy's hand tugged at Devlin's jacket.

"If you shoot me," I told Devlin, "you'll never get him downstairs and into the car. He's too big for you. And if you leave him here, he'll talk. He might go a long way for you, but he won't go to the chair for you."

A long silence followed. No argument was necessary. Devlin knew as well as I did that if he sacrificed Taffy, Taffy would say whatever he had to say.

Taffy, beside Devlin, made an effort to raise up and extricate his leg. His powerful arms leveraged him upward but the pain in his leg, aggravated by the movement, overcame him. He uttered a short cry and fell back, moaning.

But he wasn't finished yet. "Tell Cronyn to give me a hand, Devlin. And tell him to take it easy," he said between clenched teeth. In his pain he'd forgotten the "Walter."

Devlin didn't bother to look at him. He half-smiled at me and glanced at his wife. The forty-five covered both of us.

"Are you anxious to die, my dear? Would you like to be first?"

She gasped. "Walter, for God's sake. Let me go. I'll go away, so far you'll never hear from me again. Please, Walter. I don't want to die. I won't hurt you, I promise."

"I don't want you to go away," he replied. "No. As a matter of fact, I was thinking that you and I might come to an agreement."

"An agreement?"

"Yes. You agree to resume your position as my wife. In that way, you could swear that you and I spent a quiet evening at home. When the police find the bodies of these two, along with one bag of the cocaine, they will assume that each killed the other in a drug dispute." He smiled a small, cold smile in my direction. "That sort of thing occurs frequently enough, doesn't it, Cronyn?"

"It leaves you trusting her," I reminded him. "Not the greatest situation."

"I think," he replied, "that a substantial monthly alimony payment would secure her continued discretion." He turned to his wife. "Well, Paula? We haven't all night. These two must have created quite a disturbance."

It would have been a comfort to think that the police were on their way as a result of that disturbance. Taffy and I had certainly made enough noise to have wakened the neighbors, if the adjoining apartments were occupied. It hadn't lasted long, however, and the human tendency when among strangers is to roll over and go back to sleep when the noise stops. In a transient building, no one wants to become enmeshed in the lives of people you didn't know last week and will never see again.

Paula Devlin's face was gray with fear. "Yes. Yes, of course, Walter. I was a fool not to come to you immediately when this man first approached me."

I said to her. "How long do you think he will let you live?"

She ignored the question and me. It was a question that she might eventually have to face but her major concern at that moment was staying alive for another fifteen minutes.

Mine too. I had only two choices. I could stand there and take it, or I could go for him and get it. I elected to go for him in that instant when any man must hesitate when first realizing that he is about to kill another in cold blood.

Only that instant never arrived.

Taffy, behind Devlin, swept one huge arm around his boss and threw him onto the bed.

The little man squirmed in Taffy's grasp of steel. Even with Taffy hurt, Devlin was no match for that embrace. Stark fear showed from his eyes. He waved the pistol in the air and crooked his arm and pointed it behind him and fired.

The shot sounded like a paper bag filled with water hitting the sidewalk. Taffy's big body jerked with the shock of the bullet hitting his hip. A small geyser of blood erupted from the wound and subsided to a little, spurting fountain.

And then Taffy broke Devlin's neck and spine.

We talked to a lot of Virginia cops before they let us go. One of them promised to get a message through to Lieutenant Rowlson from me.

I gathered from the police who questioned me that Paula Devlin's version of the night's events and mine matched in all important respects. She'd have lied for Devlin to save herself, but the truth was better for her now. She did leave out the part about agreeing to alibi Devlin when his plan was to shoot Taffy and me. You'd expect that, I guess.

I met her in the hall where she stood with a uniformed police officer. The Virginia cops couldn't make her go with me, but they had kept her around until I could ask her myself. They were glad to be rid of her.

"I'll take you home," I told her, meaning to the house in Georgetown.

She shrank away from me. "No," she said.

"Suit yourself. They said you could go with me. They didn't say how long you'd have to wait if you didn't."

It didn't take her long to consider the consequences of that. "All right," she said. "I'll go with you." In the elevator she spoke again. "I couldn't have done anything to stop Walter."

"Forget that. You did what you had to do to stay alive. You always have."

We walked together out of the building and across the parking lot to my station wagon. If Devlin hadn't been so anxious about his cocaine, if he had just stayed in the station wagon, both he and Taffy would still have been alive and looking for lawyers.

The broken leg wouldn't have killed Taffy. Devlin's shot did. Its initial impact wasn't enough to stop a man of Taffy's strength but it tore up a major artery. There hadn't been anything I could do about Taffy's bleeding. A surgeon with all the proper equipment maybe. Not me.

Neither Paula Devlin nor I said anything until we were on Shirley Highway heading for D.C. Devlin and Taffy were behind us. Time to move on to unfinished business.

"The police detective investigating Ted Fromann's death came to see me this evening," I said. I corrected that to myself. Last evening. The earliest Friday morning commuters were already heading toward the Potomac River bridges.

"He still doesn't believe my story of a woman hiring me to go to Fromann's apartment," I went on. "He called it a fairy tale, as a matter of fact. It left me in a tough spot."

"I'm truly sorry about that. I really am."

She sounded contrite. It really didn't make any difference one way or the other, whether she was or not. When a thing is done, it's done and can't be undone.

"You will go to the police now, won't you, Mrs. Devlin? I mean, since your husband is dead, you have nothing to fear about revealing your affair with Fromann."

Silence, except for the hum of the tires on the pavement. I turned off Shirley Highway onto the George Washington Parkway. The river to our right was a vast, empty blackness.

"I suppose you're right," she answered, finally. "I'll think about it tomorrow."

"I'm afraid that you'll have to think about it now, Mrs. Devlin."

We crossed Memorial Bridge and swung around the

228

Lincoln Memorial, eerily quiet. I turned on Twenty-third and headed for Washington Circle.

"You see," I continued, "I caught up to that bus I was telling you about."

"I'm sorry," she said.

"I'm talking about the meaning of your husband's covering up for Taffy by saying that Taffy could not have followed you to Fromann's apartment last Saturday."

Silence from the seat beside me. She knew what I meant. She just wanted to hear me say it, to be sure.

"Taffy didn't follow you," I went on, "on Saturday. He was following you on Monday, when you came to my office." I paused. "After you'd been to see Fromann."

I negotiated Washington Circle and headed toward Georgetown. She didn't seem inclined to talk so I did.

"You knew that I'd figure that out, eventually. Maybe you realized that even while you were in my office yesterday. That's why you set me up at the Twenty Grand. I was getting too close. Getting back into Devlin's good graces was a second benefit. What you really wanted was for Taffy to shoot me."

"Are you making this up as you go along?" she asked. Her voice held a note of sarcasm in it.

"No good, Mrs. Devlin," I responded. "It all fits. Someone left the door to Fromann's apartment purposefully ajar, to make it easy for me to discover the body. Only you knew with certainty that I'd be going there. Another thing. The money. Later, when I learned what sort of business your husband had going, I could understand why you had been so anxious on Monday afternoon to put the ten grand back into his safe. You didn't dare let him know you had the combination."

"I hope you're nearly finished," she said. "We're almost there."

"Almost," I said. "Your problem was that you had to have the money to give your story credibility, and you had no place else to get that much. What I couldn't figure out was what you'd have done if I had actually handed the money over to Fromann."

"This is the street," she said.

I turned. "Of course," I said, "how to explain the missing ten thou had never been a problem for you. You knew that Fromann wouldn't be needing it when you went to his place."

I slowed. Ahead was the townhouse where she'd lived eight years of her life. Parked cars lined both sides of the dark, still street. Ahead, about where the Devlin house stood, a dark sedan was double-parked, tail lights blinking. I pulled up behind it.

"You went there," I went on, "with the intention of murdering Ted Fromann. And you did."

We faced each other. The glow of the dark lights gave only a shadowy view of her face, her lips black, her eyes shadowed.

"You have no proof," she said. "Nothing."

"No," I admitted.

"I could accuse you of extortion," she added. "You would have no defense."

"I could tell about the letters," I reminded her.

I thought that I could almost see her smile. "Yes," she said. "The letters."

Two men in dark raincoats left the sedan ahead of us and walked in our direction.

I turned toward Paula Devlin. "Police," I told her. "I can't prove any of it, can I, Mrs. Devlin? Because those letters existed only in your imagination."

230

20

LIEUTENANT ROWLSON AND Detective Karle stood with Paula Devlin and me in the Devlin living room, the small room with the antiques and the flowery rug.

Rowlson looked at Paula Devlin. "Cronyn asked the Alexandria police to contact me. He told them that you are the woman who had been Ted Fromann's lover, and that Fromann was blackmailing you over some letters. He says that you hired him to buy them from Fromann. Is that correct?"

"May I sit, Lieutenant?" she asked, plaintively. He nodded, and she sat down in the same chair Devlin had used two nights earlier, when he had given me a choice of leaving town or dying.

Paula Devlin looked up at Rowlson. "I don't know if I'm coherent or not, Lieutenant," she said. "This night has been a succession of horrors."

"I understand, Mrs. Devlin," said Rowlson. He looked sympathetic. "Whatever you can tell us would be appreciated."

She took a deep breath. She looked sincere. She always looked sincere when she wanted to. "I had never met this man," she said, meaning me, "until several days ago. He approached me with a demand for ten thousand dollars. He said that if I did not give it to him he would go to the police with that story about some letters and the rest. He said a murder was involved and that he had already told the same lie to the police."

"That's extortion, Mrs. Devlin. It's a serious accusation."

She closed her eyes and swayed on the chair. "Oh God," she breathed. "I can still see my husband like . . . like that." She opened her eyes wide and looked at me. "He told me I had better agree to tell that story when we arrived here. I was so afraid, Lieutenant. I agreed, of course. Thank God you were here when we arrived. He might have . . . done anything to me."

Rowlson looked at me. It wasn't suspicion so much as anger I saw in his eyes. He was remembering Al Paddock. So was I.

I went and sat down. "Tell you a story," I said to him. "It's not a long story, but it goes back a long time." I felt tired, very tired, and more than a little old. I thought about people I was sure I had forgotten, and some that I wished I could forget.

I thought about little Harvey Koppel and the man who called himself Blasingame now and the woman who had been a flower child at the beginning of time and who now sat beside an empty chair in her kitchen.

"There were four kids who played with nitroglycerin," I went on. "Trina, Jenny, Mike, and Robbie. They wanted to change the world."

Detective Karle spoke up. "That's those bombers who blew themselves up, Lieutenant. Remember I told you that Cronyn cocked around in all that radical crap."

I ignored the comment and continued. "After that explosion, those associated with the bombings went underground. A story began circulating that one person had escaped from the house before it blew up. No one in the underground believed the story. They all thought it was an FBI plant. The exception was Ted Fromann. He believed the story because he wanted to believe the girl he loved was still alive."

"Maybe we ought to go downtown," said Rowlson, "and let Mrs. Devlin try to sleep."

"This won't take long," I assured him. "Anyway, Fromann spread the word of his whereabouts so his girlfriend could find him. The FBI found him instead. He escaped and had been a fugitive ever since. His old buddies thought the FBI had made a fool of him. He may have thought so, too." I paused. "That is, until he came to Washington, where he met someone who had something interesting to tell him."

"Does this person have a name?" asked Rowlson.

"Call her Daffodil," I said. "She lives in a half-world peopled by ghosts and guilts. She and Fromann would have talked about the bombers, surely. They each lost someone dear to them in the explosion."

"What did she have to tell Fromann?" asked Rowlson.

"This. On the morning of the explosion, she had called her lover, Trina. Jenny answered the telephone. Daffodil and Trina had had a quarrel the night before. They talked at length, trying to make it up. Mike became angry because he was expecting a call. Daffodil could hear him shouting at Trina to get off the telephone. Abruptly the phone went dead. The house had blown up, killing all those inside at the time."

"So what did that story mean to Fromann?" asked Rowlson.

"It must have confirmed what he originally believed, that is, that one of the four escaped."

Rowlson wrinkled his forehead as he worked through the unfamiliar names. "Robbie?" he offered. "He's the only one you didn't mention being there."

I shook my head. "His body was positively identified."

Rowlson protested. "Then nobody could have missed it. They were all there."

"Trina and Mike were there," I agreed, "but Jenny Whalen had plenty of time during that phone call to leave the house after initially answering it. And then Daffodil confirmed it. She had seen Jenny Whalen, alive and well and shopping in Woodies' downtown store several years ago. She'd raised quite a fuss over seeing the ghost, as she thought of it. No one took her seriously, and the store was glad that the customer, a valued one, never knew about it."

"And Fromann believed this story about a ghost?" asked Rowlson, sounding skeptical.

"He believed it years ago, at the risk of prison," I answered. "Why not now?"

Rowlson nodded his reluctant agreement. "She'd be using another name," he said. "Those bombers were wanted in a dozen states. If the FBI had caught any of them, they'd have thrown the key away."

"Yes," I said. It was motive enough for murder. "Daffodil wouldn't have known the name, but Fromann could have reasoned that such a valued customer would return to the store. So he staked it out."

"Jeez, Lieutenant," said Karle, his eyes rounding. "We found a half-dozen Woodies' shopping bags in Fromann's apartment."

Rowlson stared at me. "He found Jenny Whalen."

"Yes. And he could easily have discovered the name she was using."

The Westminster clock chimes played for me again. Rowlson said nothing, showed nothing. Karle shifted his glance between the two of us. Paula Devlin sat rigid and white-faced on her chair.

Finally Rowlson asked the question. "What is the name?"

"Mrs. Walter Devlin," I replied.

Rowlson came to see me late Friday afternoon. "The Thresher woman took her sister to Ohio," he said.

"Yeah."

"She called you?" he asked.

"That's right. I told her just to get on the plane and go."

She hadn't wanted to go, she'd told me. Too many things seemed to have been left unsaid between us.

I put that thought away and spoke to Rowlson again.

"Not a whole lot you could do about it, since she was in Maryland, not D.C."

"You do know how to make friends, don't you?" he said. He looked around the office and then back to me. "We got a match on the fingerprints. How did you figure Paula Devlin to be Jenny Whalen?"

I told him about Taffy following her to Fromann's place and about the money. "That made her the best bet for killing him. Another thing that didn't sit right with me was how she and Fromann had connected. It seemed too coincidental."

"That was before you knew that Salamonica had pointed Fromann in her direction."

"Yes. If I had known that . . . ," I didn't finish the thought. "Those damned letters kept getting in the way. Why come to me, if she'd already killed Fromann?"

Rowlson didn't think that was too hard to understand. "She wanted everyone to think that she had *not* killed him."

"Then why come to me at all? If she had shot him and taken the letters, why tell me about the letters and the blackmail at all? Telling me simply gave her a motive for killing him. She didn't have to do that, especially since there had never been any letters."

He wrinkled his smooth, chestnut forehead. "You were pretty sure of them, as I hear it."

"I was sure, same as I'm sure that I have more or less brown hair," I replied. "But if a dozen people tell you that your hair is turning green, you'd better look in the mirror. That's what I did last night, and I saw myself standing there all alone. I was the only one who believed in the existence of those letters, and the only evidence I had of them was what Paula Devlin told me.

"So I turned that around and considered the possibility that she had lied, that she had not had an affair with Fromann and had not written any letters. But I also told myself that nobody invents a motive for murder."

"Unless," said Rowlson, "she needed it in order to cover up her real motive. It wasn't Murray Atwood blackmailing Paula Devlin. It was Ted Fromann blackmailing Jenny Whalen."

"Right, Lieutenant. She was vulnerable. Fromann could threaten to expose her without coming forward himself. Even an anonymous letter to the FBI would have put them on her trail. She had to keep him quiet. But she had no money, not what he was demanding, at least."

"She must have given him some," Rowlson said, "for him to set up in that apartment."

"She had to string him along until she decided what to do about him. She probably gave him a few hundred of her own at a time. After she decided to kill him, she realized that witnesses to those visits might turn up. If the police located her, she needed to have a reason for those visits. She needed a reason for her to be connected to Murray Atwood, not Ted Fromann."

"She could have told us," Rowlson observed.

"Sure, but would you have had to believe her? She wanted someone to back her story up, someone who could say that he'd seen the evidence that those letters existed, that is, the ten thousand dollars with which she planned to buy back those non-existent letters."

"So if she wanted an alibi, why didn't she use it?"

"I was her alibi only in the event that she needed one. If your people had caught up to her, she would have told her story of passion betrayed."

"Reluctantly," observed Rowlson.

"Of course. That was part of the act," I replied. "Since she didn't need me, she left me to twist slowly in the breeze."

236

"They once were lovers, she and Fromann."

"Yes," I said. "In his mind, she had betrayed him by not coming to him or letting him know that she was still alive after the explosion. He had lost too much, too many years gone, as a result of that betrayal, for love to survive."

I could almost visualize her sitting there where Rowlson sat. I could almost hear her telling me once again that she had reminded the dead man of what they once meant to each other. I was supposed to think that referred to the false affair, but for a moment there had been reality in her voice. She probably had pleaded with him, invoking their young love. But just as he had lost too much, she had gained too much. Her voice had hardened then. "According to what she told me," I continued, "it all came down to a question of money." The words sounded strange to me as I said them, almost like an echo.

"Yeah," he said without emotion. "It usually does." He stood up. So far neither of us had said anything about Paddock, which was all right by me. He looked around the office. I guess he hadn't noticed much the night before.

"How's business?" he asked.

"Not bad."

"Captain suggested that maybe you should steer clear of homicide cases in the future."

"I'll try. No money in them."

"Yeah." He hesitated. "If it doesn't always work out that way, Cronyn, might be a good idea if you checked in with me, personally."

"Was that the Captain's idea?"

He almost smiled. Almost. I wondered if homicide cops ever smiled.

"Mine," he said. "Take it easy, Cronyn." He left, shutting the door after him.

I sat there for a moment, listening for the elevator and staring at the closed door. I'd be seeing Lieutenant Rowlson again, I supposed, because the only way to shut the door on the cops is if they do it themselves.

Epilogue

CHARLIE HODES BROUGHT some of the old bunch together for Christmas dinner, some of those whom we'd known best. We ate turkey and all the fixings at a restaurant in Arlington run by a clan of Vietnamese refugees, and we talked about the last election and the next one, about Central America and South Africa and all the things you'd think aging radicals might talk about. Nobody wanted to talk about Jenny Whalen and Ted Fromann even though it had been on the front page of the papers the week before.

It snowed Christmas night. The next morning I looked out upon a line of traffic on New Hampshire Avenue and upon pedestrians wrapped against the cold. I decided to take some vacation time.

I read and watched TV and napped the day away. Late in the afternoon the telephone rang.

It was the guy at the desk downstairs. "Mary Thresher to see you," he announced.

I told him to send her up. I met her at the door. She had a small suitcase. I took it and set it in front of the TV, which I turned off. She gave me her coat and sat down.

"How's Dilly?" I asked. I sat across from her.

"She's fine. She likes the place she's at. She spent all day yesterday at home. It was almost like . . . ," her voice trailed off. Dilly wasn't better. Dilly would never get better. Love and care were the best she could hope for, and I guessed that she had it.

"And you?"

239

She gave me a little smile. "Okay. I had to come back to clear out the apartment. I couldn't get a cab driver at the airport to take me out to Maryland because of the snow, so I came here." She looked around. "It hasn't changed any," she said. She looked back to me. "I'm going back to Ohio. I don't want to stay in this city."

"Yeah," I replied. I wanted her to know that I understood. She wasn't running away. She had come to my town to do that.

"I'm going out into the world and see if anybody likes me," she said. A pause. "I can't hide behind Dilly any longer."

I didn't say anything. Neither of us did.

"I'm scared," she said, at last. She didn't look at me.

I wondered if she still felt as though too many things had been left unsaid between us, as though we had our own song to finish before life could resume again. I wanted her to stay but I didn't know how to put it into words so I just stood up and went to the TV and took her bag from there into the bedroom. When I returned to the living room, I asked, "Blackie's for dinner?"

Her eyes held mine for a moment before she answered. "I'd like that," she said, quietly.

We had dinners together and breakfasts together, and in between we made love. It began tentatively, as though we were starting our song all over from the beginning. Then it turned sure and full and rich as her confidence grew. We ice skated on the Mall, and we explored the National Gallery of Art, and we walked hand in hand along the ice-fringed Potomac. At first she talked about everything in her life, releasing a torrent of pent-up thoughts. As the hours of our togetherness wound down, she grew more silent. In those moments, she withdrew from me, psyching herself for the moment when she felt ready to leave.

That moment came on the morning of the fourth day.

240

Our song had ended; our separate lives were ready to begin again. I took her to the airport.

She wavered then and looked up at me with uncertainty in her eyes. "It was good," she said, "these last few days. Time suspended. But we can't suspend time forever, can we, Dan? We have to go on, looking for what's right for us, even when it means taking chances." For a moment she squeezed my hand. Then she turned away without a word.

I watched her pass through the security portal, as though she were crossing the threshold to something very new and exciting. On the other side, she turned and waved and the smile she showed me said that she'd do just fine.

If you have enjoyed this book and would like to receive details of other Walker mystery titles, please write to:

Mystery Editor
Walker and Company
720 Fifth Avenue
New York, NY 10019